D0606436

KRYPTO
The SUPERDOG™

SUPERMAN CREATED BY
JERRY SIEGEL AND JOE SHUSTER
BY SPECIAL ARRANGEMENT WITH
THE JERRY SIEGEL FAMILY

STONE ARCH BOOKS
a capstone imprint

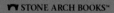 STONE ARCH BOOKS™

Published in 2014
A Capstone Imprint
1710 Roe Crest Drive
North Mankato, MN 56003
www.capstonepub.com

Originally published by DC Comics in the U.S. in single magazine form as
Kryto The Superdog #2. Copyright © 2014 DC Comics. All Rights Reserved.

DC Comics
1700 Broadway, New York, NY 10019
A Warner Bros. Entertainment Company

No part of this publication may be reproduced in whole or in part, or stored in a retrieval
system, or transmitted in any form or by any means, electronic, mechanical, photocopying,
recording, or otherwise, without written permission.

Cataloging-in-Publication Data is available at the
Library of Congress website
ISBN: 978-1-4342-6471-8 (library binding)

Summary: It's a crisis for Krypto as he and his friend, Kevin, travel to different dimensions!
But will everyone they meet be as friendly and helpful as the Super Pup himself?

STONE ARCH BOOKS
Ashley C. Andersen Zantop Publisher
Michael Dahl Editorial Director
Donald Lemke & Sean Tulien Editors
Bob Lentz Art Director
Hilary Wacholz Designer

DC COMICS
Kristy Quinn Original U.S. Editor

Printed in China by Nordica.
1013 / CA21301918
092013   007744NORDS14

KRYPTO

THE SUPERDOG ™

Crisis of Infinite Kryptos

JESSE LEON McCANN...................................WRITER

MIN. S. KU ....PENCILLER

JEFF ALBRECHT .... INKER

DAVE TANGUAY ....COLORIST

DAVE TANGUAY ....LETTERER

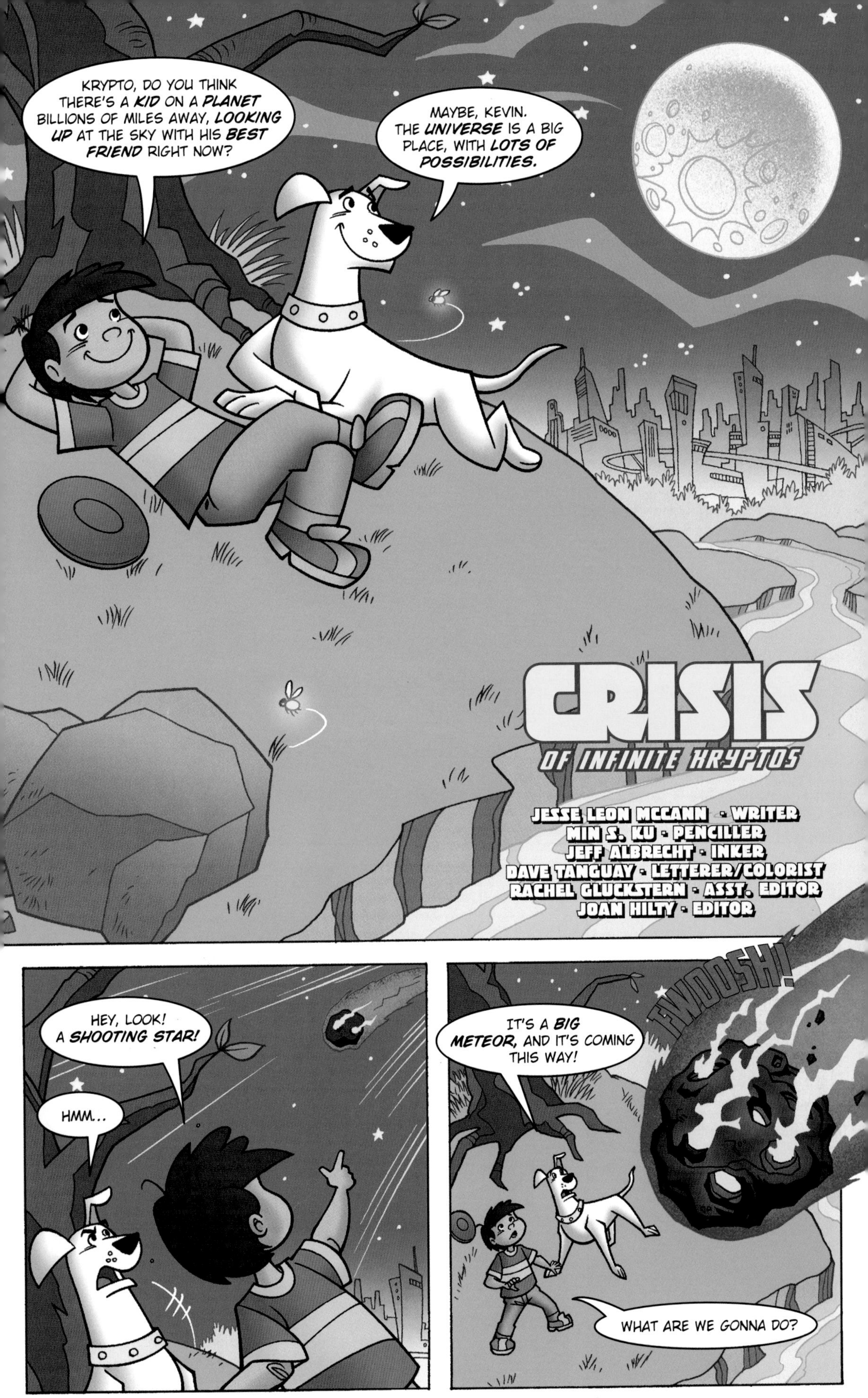
KRYPTO, DO YOU THINK THERE'S A KID ON A PLANET BILLIONS OF MILES AWAY, LOOKING UP AT THE SKY WITH HIS BEST FRIEND RIGHT NOW?
MAYBE, KEVIN. THE UNIVERSE IS A BIG PLACE, WITH LOTS OF POSSIBILITIES.
CRISIS
OF INFINITE KRYPTOS
JESSE LEON McCANN - WRITER
MIN S. KU - PENCILLER
JEFF ALBRECHT - INKER
DAVE TANGUAY - LETTERER/COLORIST
RACHEL GLUCKSTERN - ASST. EDITOR
JOAN HILTY - EDITOR
HEY, LOOK! A SHOOTING STAR!
HMM..
FWOOSH!
IT'S A BIG METEOR, AND IT'S COMING THIS WAY!
WHAT ARE WE GONNA DO?

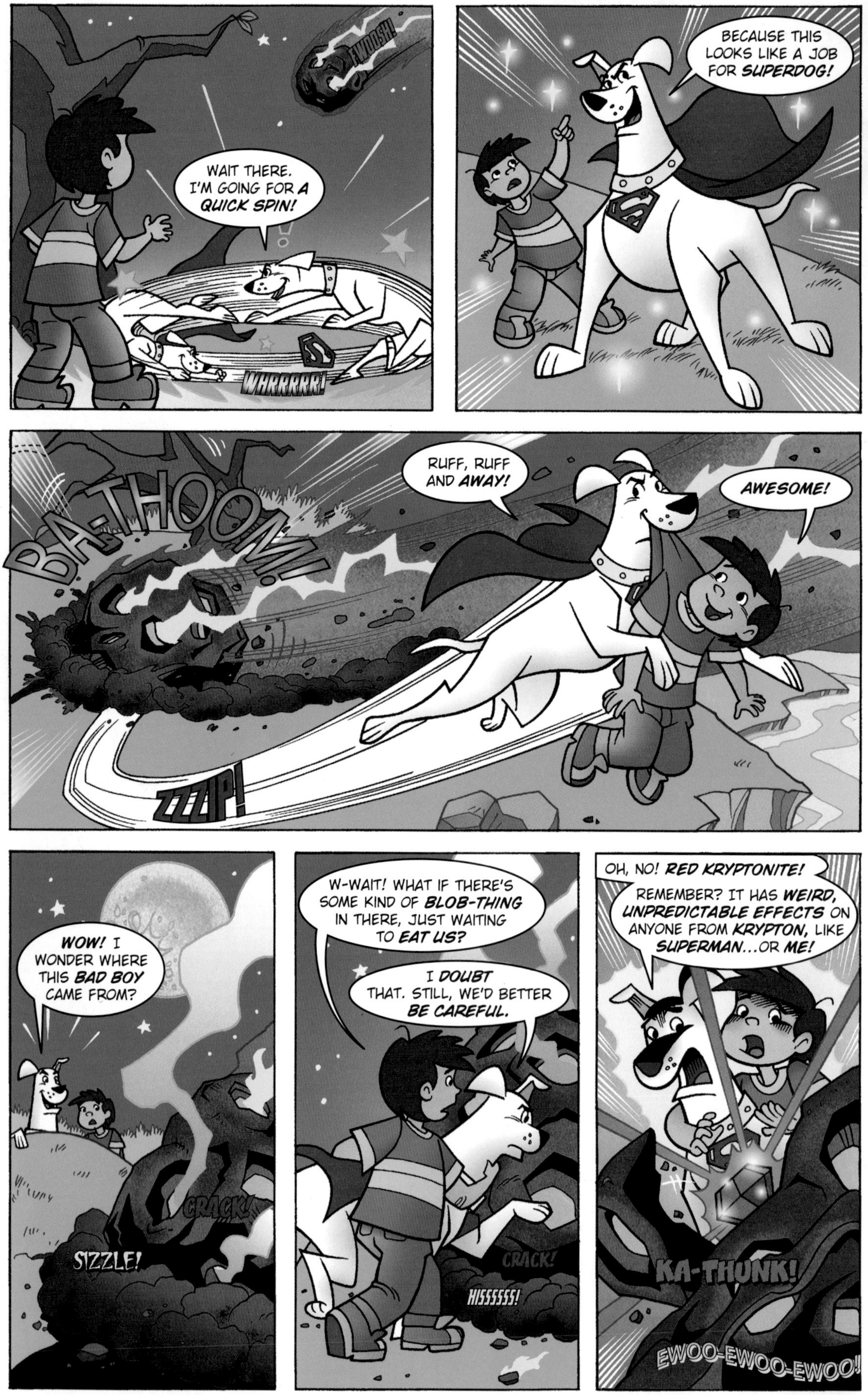
FWOOSH!
WAIT THERE. I'M GOING FOR A QUICK SPIN!
WHRRRRR!
BECAUSE THIS LOOKS LIKE A JOB FOR SUPERDOG!
BA-THOOM!
RUFF, RUFF AND AWAY!
AWESOME!
ZZZIP!
WOW! I WONDER WHERE THIS BAD BOY CAME FROM?
CRACK!
SIZZLE!
W-WAIT! WHAT IF THERE'S SOME KIND OF BLOB-THING IN THERE, JUST WAITING TO EAT US?
I DOUBT THAT. STILL, WE'D BETTER BE CAREFUL.
CRACK!
HISSSSSS!
OH, NO! RED KRYPTONITE!
REMEMBER? IT HAS WEIRD, UNPREDICTABLE EFFECTS ON ANYONE FROM KRYPTON, LIKE SUPERMAN...OR ME!
KA-THUNK!
EWOO-EWOO-EWOO!

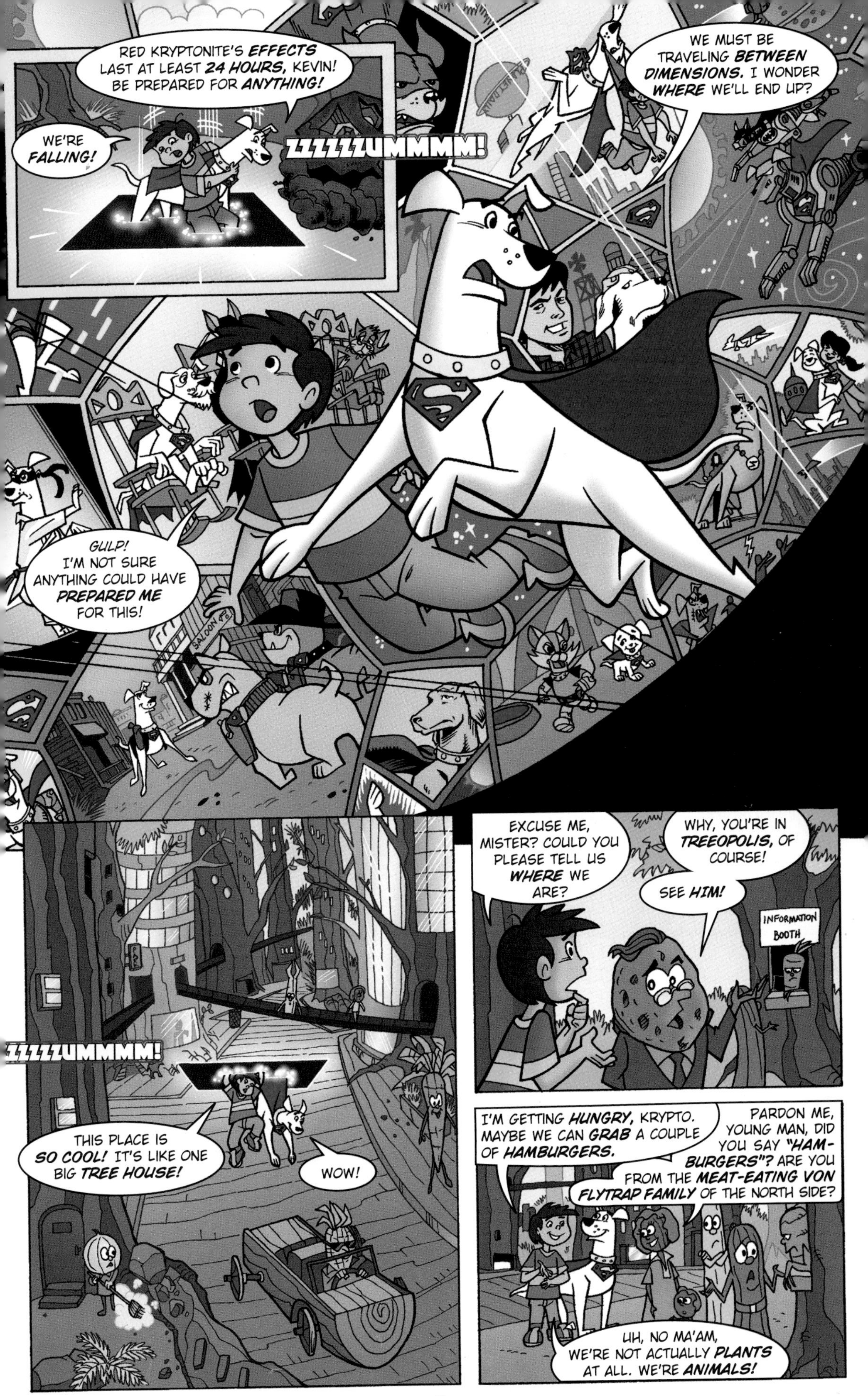
RED KRYPTONITE'S EFFECTS LAST AT LEAST 24 HOURS, KEVIN! BE PREPARED FOR ANYTHING!
WE'RE FALLING!
ZZZZZZUMMMMM!
WE MUST BE TRAVELING BETWEEN DIMENSIONS. I WONDER WHERE WE'LL END UP?
GULP! I'M NOT SURE ANYTHING COULD HAVE PREPARED ME FOR THIS!
SALOON
ZZZZZUMMMMM!
THIS PLACE IS SO COOL! IT'S LIKE ONE BIG TREE HOUSE!
WOW!
EXCUSE ME, MISTER? COULD YOU PLEASE TELL US WHERE WE ARE?
WHY, YOU'RE IN TREEOPOLIS, OF COURSE!
SEE HIM!
INFORMATION BOOTH
I'M GETTING HUNGRY, KRYPTO. MAYBE WE CAN GRAB A COUPLE OF HAMBURGERS.
PARDON ME, YOUNG MAN, DID YOU SAY "HAM-BURGERS"? ARE YOU FROM THE MEAT-EATING VON FLYTRAP FAMILY OF THE NORTH SIDE?
UH, NO MA'AM, WE'RE NOT ACTUALLY PLANTS AT ALL. WE'RE ANIMALS!

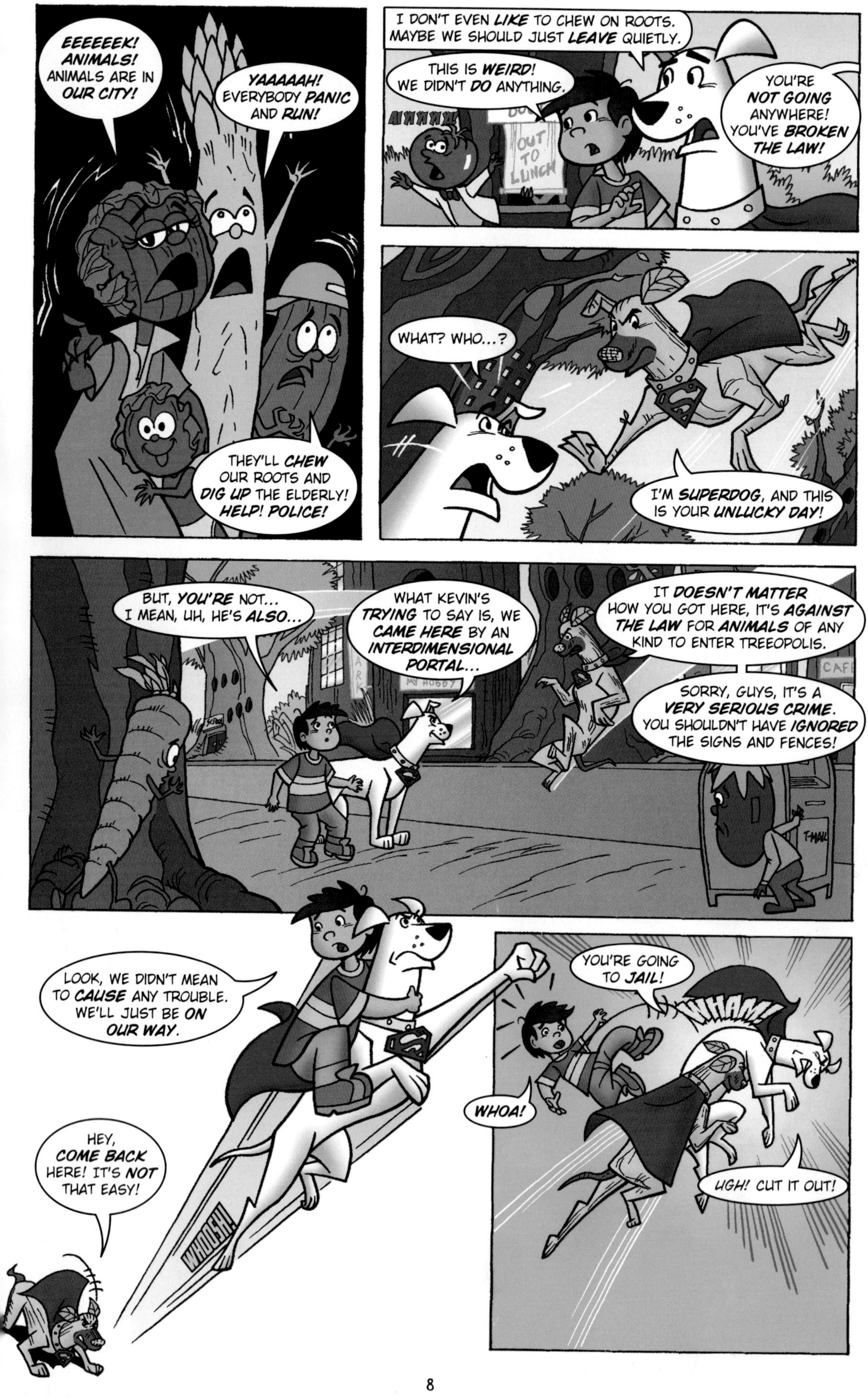
EEEEEEK! ANIMALS! ANIMALS ARE IN OUR CITY!
YAAAAAH! EVERYBODY PANIC AND RUN!
THEY'LL CHEW OUR ROOTS AND DIG UP THE ELDERLY! HELP! POLICE!
I DON'T EVEN LIKE TO CHEW ON ROOTS. MAYBE WE SHOULD JUST LEAVE QUIETLY.
THIS IS WEIRD! WE DIDN'T DO ANYTHING.
YOU'RE NOT GOING ANYWHERE! YOU'VE BROKEN THE LAW!
OUT TO LUNCH
WHAT? WHO...?
I'M SUPERDOG, AND THIS IS YOUR UNLUCKY DAY!
BUT, YOU'RE NOT... I MEAN, UH, HE'S ALSO...
WHAT KEVIN'S TRYING TO SAY IS, WE CAME HERE BY AN INTERDIMENSIONAL PORTAL...
IT DOESN'T MATTER HOW YOU GOT HERE, IT'S AGAINST THE LAW FOR ANIMALS OF ANY KIND TO ENTER TREEOPOLIS.
SORRY, GUYS, IT'S A VERY SERIOUS CRIME. YOU SHOULDN'T HAVE IGNORED THE SIGNS AND FENCES!
LOOK, WE DIDN'T MEAN TO CAUSE ANY TROUBLE. WE'LL JUST BE ON OUR WAY.
HEY, COME BACK HERE! IT'S NOT THAT EASY!
WHOOSH!
YOU'RE GOING TO JAIL!
WHAM!
WHOA!
UGH! CUT IT OUT!

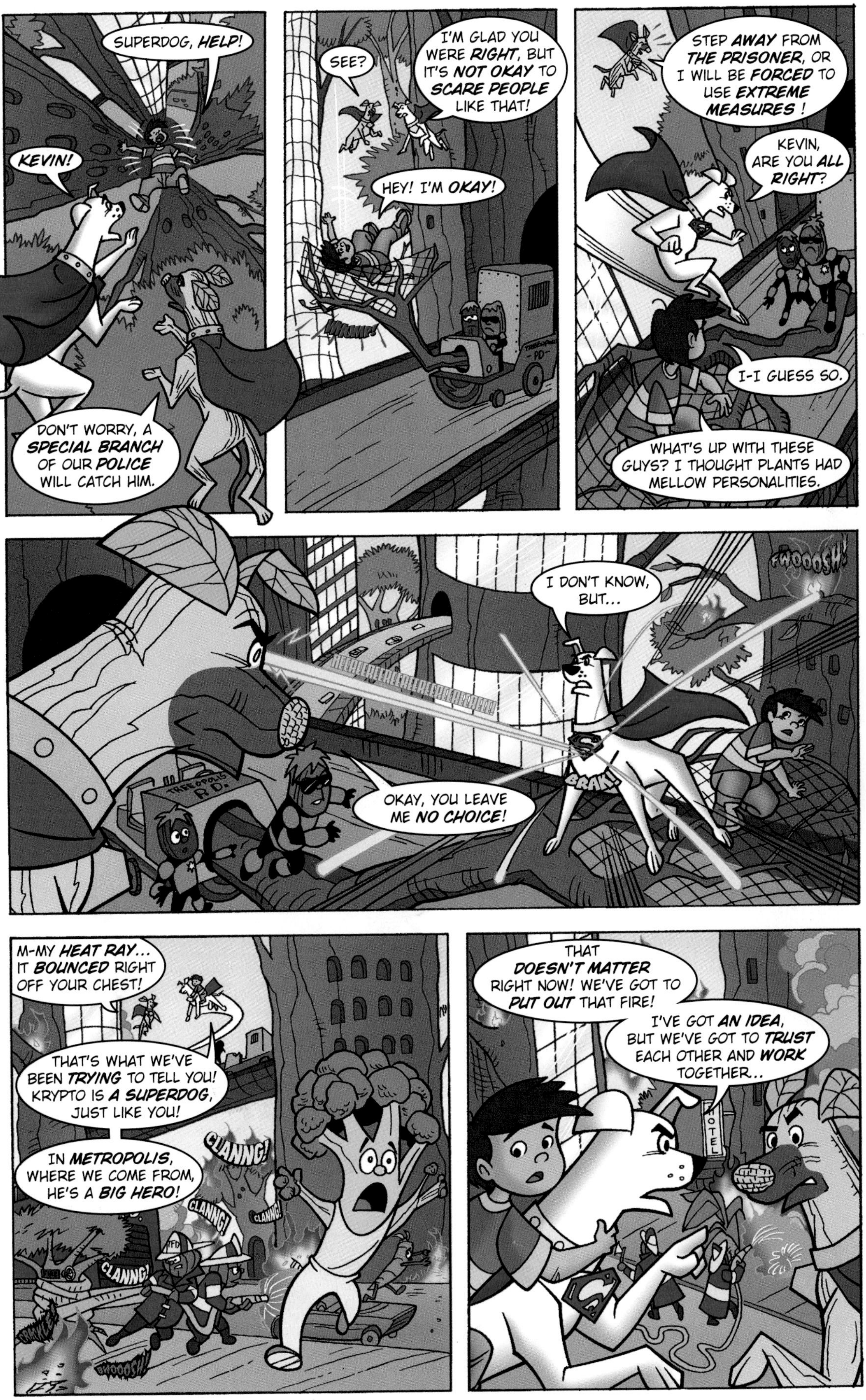
SUPERDOG, HELP!
KEVIN!
DON'T WORRY, A SPECIAL BRANCH OF OUR POLICE WILL CATCH HIM.
SEE?
I'M GLAD YOU WERE RIGHT, BUT IT'S NOT OKAY TO SCARE PEOPLE LIKE THAT!
HEY! I'M OKAY!
STEP AWAY FROM THE PRISONER, OR I WILL BE FORCED TO USE EXTREME MEASURES !
KEVIN, ARE YOU ALL RIGHT?
I-I GUESS SO.
WHAT'S UP WITH THESE GUYS? I THOUGHT PLANTS HAD MELLOW PERSONALITIES.
FWOOOSH!
I DON'T KNOW, BUT...
TREEOPOLIS P.D.
OKAY, YOU LEAVE ME NO CHOICE!
BRAK!
M-MY HEAT RAY... IT BOUNCED RIGHT OFF YOUR CHEST!
THAT'S WHAT WE'VE BEEN TRYING TO TELL YOU! KRYPTO IS A SUPERDOG, JUST LIKE YOU!
IN METROPOLIS, WHERE WE COME FROM, HE'S A BIG HERO!
CLANNG!
CLANNG!
CLANNG!
CLANNG!
THAT DOESN'T MATTER RIGHT NOW! WE'VE GOT TO PUT OUT THAT FIRE!
I'VE GOT AN IDEA, BUT WE'VE GOT TO TRUST EACH OTHER AND WORK TOGETHER..
HOTEL

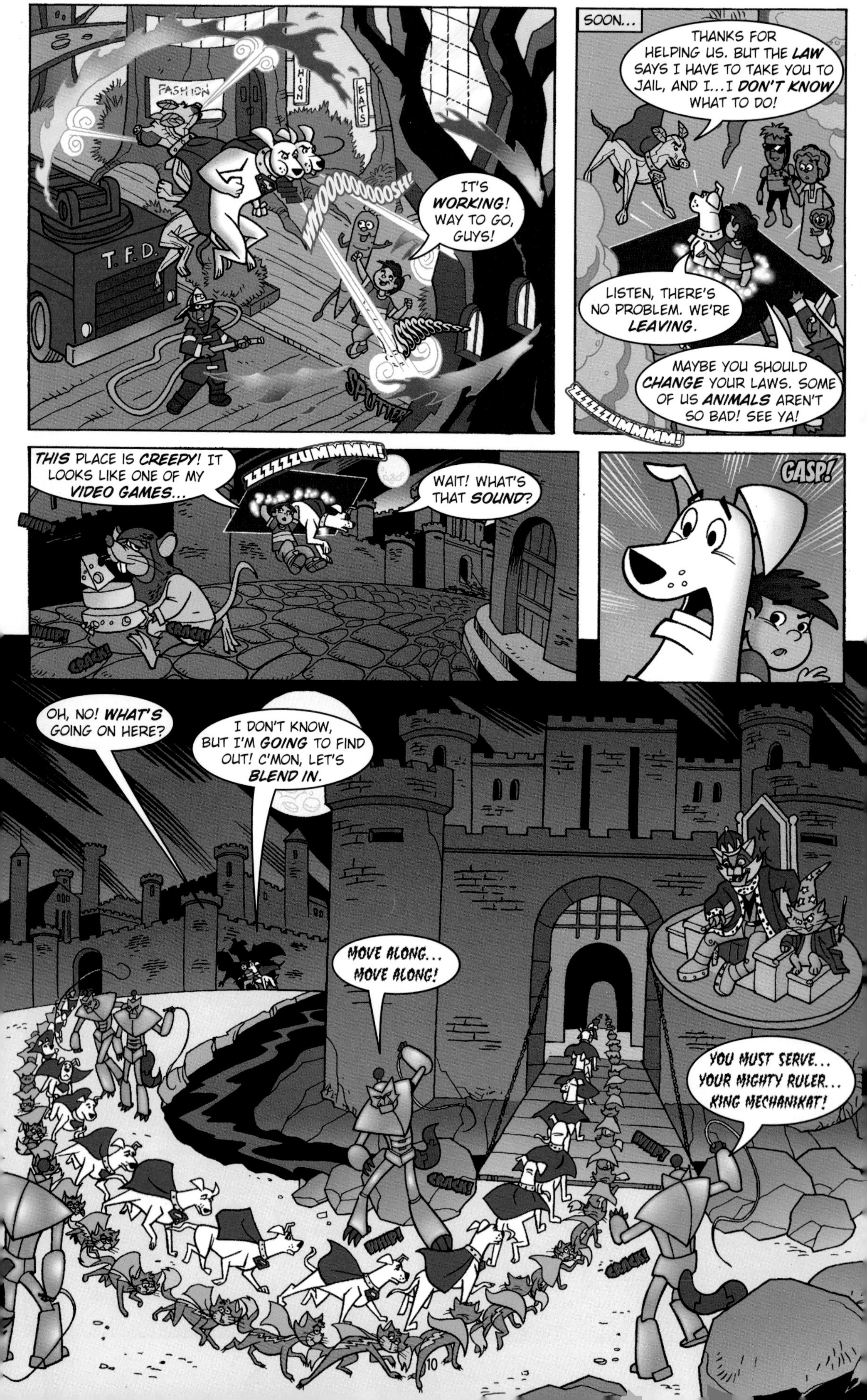

FASHION
HION
EATS
T.F.D.
WHOOOOOOOOOOSH!
IT'S WORKING! WAY TO GO, GUYS!
SSSSSSSS!
SPUTTER!
SOON...
THANKS FOR HELPING US. BUT THE LAW SAYS I HAVE TO TAKE YOU TO JAIL, AND I...I DON'T KNOW WHAT TO DO!
LISTEN, THERE'S NO PROBLEM. WE'RE LEAVING.
MAYBE YOU SHOULD CHANGE YOUR LAWS. SOME OF US ANIMALS AREN'T SO BAD! SEE YA!
ZZZZZZZUMMMMM!
THIS PLACE IS CREEPY! IT LOOKS LIKE ONE OF MY VIDEO GAMES...
ZZZZZZUMMMM!
WAIT! WHAT'S THAT SOUND?
WHIP!
CRACK!
GASP!
OH, NO! WHAT'S GOING ON HERE?
I DON'T KNOW, BUT I'M GOING TO FIND OUT! C'MON, LET'S BLEND IN.
MOVE ALONG... MOVE ALONG!
YOU MUST SERVE... YOUR MIGHTY RULER... KING MECHANIKAT!
CRACK!
WHIP!

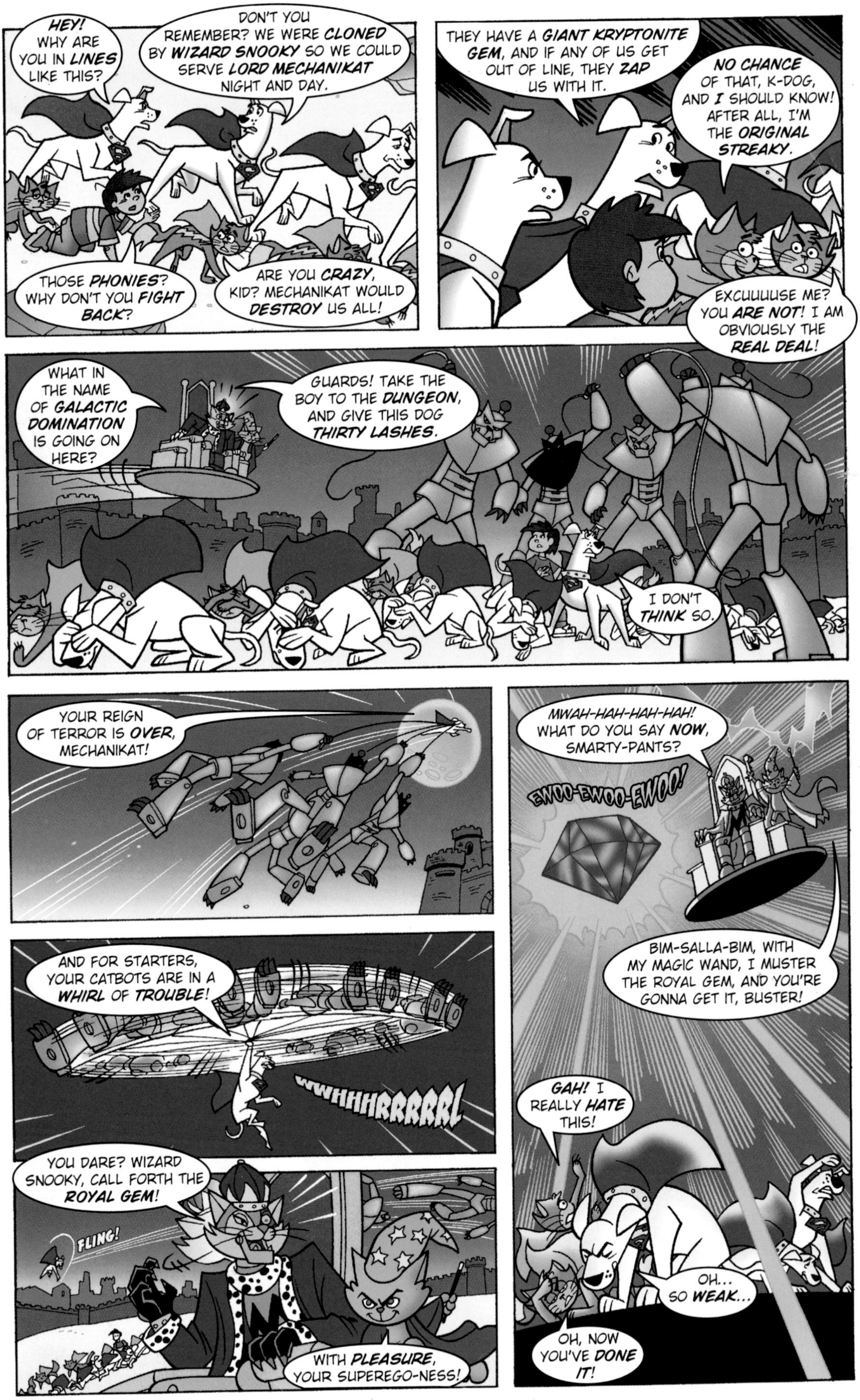
HEY! WHY ARE YOU IN LINES LIKE THIS?
DON'T YOU REMEMBER? WE WERE CLONED BY WIZARD SNOOKY SO WE COULD SERVE LORD MECHANIKAT NIGHT AND DAY.
THOSE PHONIES? WHY DON'T YOU FIGHT BACK?
ARE YOU CRAZY, KID? MECHANIKAT WOULD DESTROY US ALL!
THEY HAVE A GIANT KRYPTONITE GEM, AND IF ANY OF US GET OUT OF LINE, THEY ZAP US WITH IT.
NO CHANCE OF THAT, K-DOG, AND I SHOULD KNOW! AFTER ALL, I'M THE ORIGINAL STREAKY.
EXCUUUUSE ME? YOU ARE NOT! I AM OBVIOUSLY THE REAL DEAL!
WHAT IN THE NAME OF GALACTIC DOMINATION IS GOING ON HERE?
GUARDS! TAKE THE BOY TO THE DUNGEON, AND GIVE THIS DOG THIRTY LASHES.
I DON'T THINK SO.
YOUR REIGN OF TERROR IS OVER, MECHANIKAT!
AND FOR STARTERS, YOUR CATBOTS ARE IN A WHIRL OF TROUBLE!
WWHHHRRRRRL
YOU DARE? WIZARD SNOOKY, CALL FORTH THE ROYAL GEM!
FLING!
WITH PLEASURE, YOUR SUPEREGO-NESS!
MWAH-HAH-HAH-HAH! WHAT DO YOU SAY NOW, SMARTY-PANTS?
EWOO-EWOO-EWOO!
BIM-SALLA-BIM, WITH MY MAGIC WAND, I MUSTER THE ROYAL GEM, AND YOU'RE GONNA GET IT, BUSTER!
GAH! I REALLY HATE THIS!
OH... SO WEAK...
OH, NOW YOU'VE DONE IT!

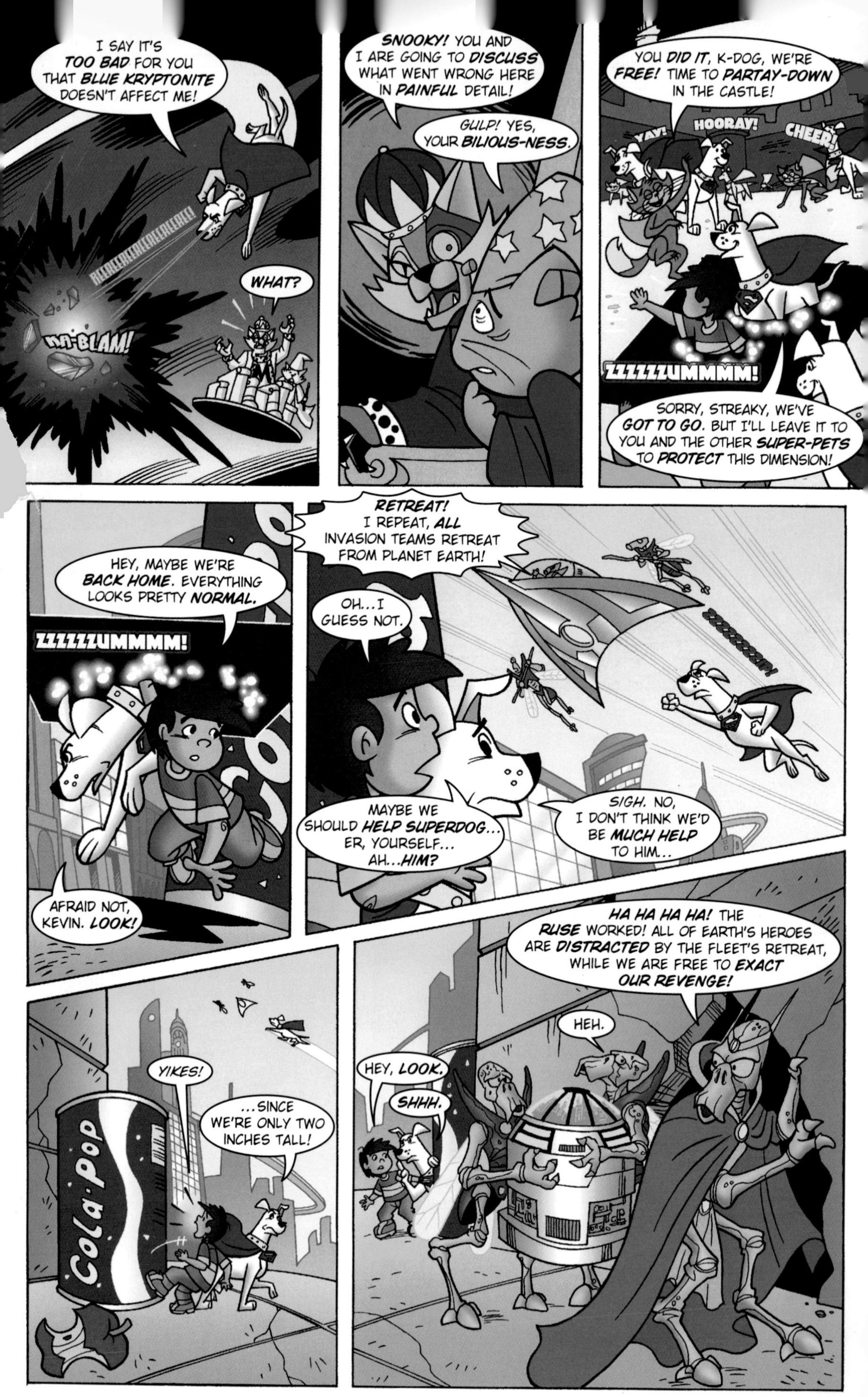
I SAY IT'S TOO BAD FOR YOU THAT BLUE KRYPTONITE DOESN'T AFFECT ME!
KA-BLAM!
WHAT?
SNOOKY! YOU AND I ARE GOING TO DISCUSS WHAT WENT WRONG HERE IN PAINFUL DETAIL!
GULP! YES, YOUR BILIOUS-NESS.
YOU DID IT, K-DOG, WE'RE FREE! TIME TO PARTAY-DOWN IN THE CASTLE!
YAY!
HOORAY!
CHEER!
ZZZZZZUMMMM!
SORRY, STREAKY, WE'VE GOT TO GO. BUT I'LL LEAVE IT TO YOU AND THE OTHER SUPER-PETS TO PROTECT THIS DIMENSION!
HEY, MAYBE WE'RE BACK HOME. EVERYTHING LOOKS PRETTY NORMAL.
ZZZZZZUMMMM!
AFRAID NOT, KEVIN. LOOK!
RETREAT! I REPEAT, ALL INVASION TEAMS RETREAT FROM PLANET EARTH!
OH...I GUESS NOT.
MAYBE WE SHOULD HELP SUPERDOG... ER, YOURSELF... AH...HIM?
SIGH. NO, I DON'T THINK WE'D BE MUCH HELP TO HIM...
YIKES!
...SINCE WE'RE ONLY TWO INCHES TALL!
Cola-Pop
HA HA HA HA! THE RUSE WORKED! ALL OF EARTH'S HEROES ARE DISTRACTED BY THE FLEET'S RETREAT, WHILE WE ARE FREE TO EXACT OUR REVENGE!
HEH.
HEY, LOOK.
SHHH.

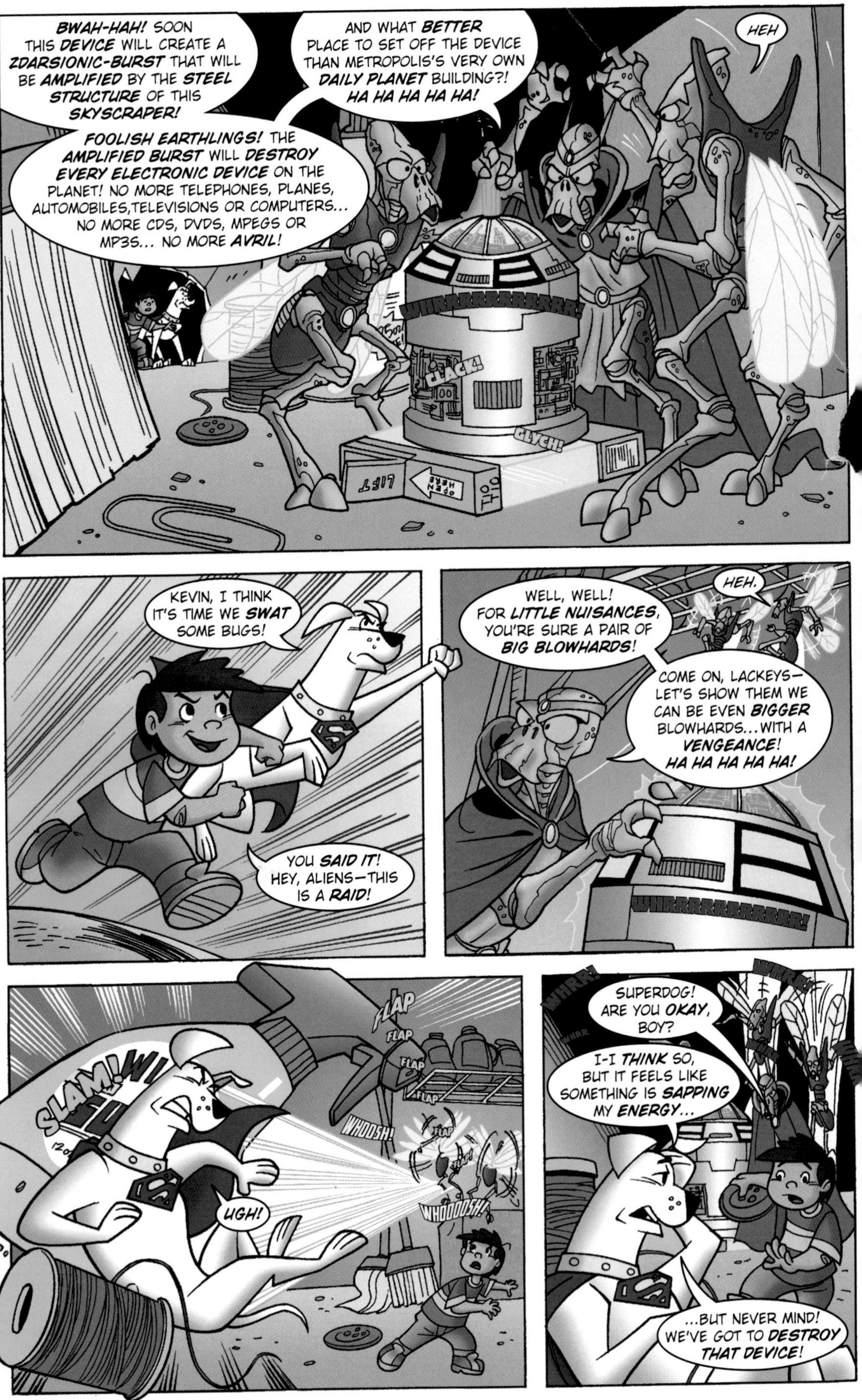
BWAH-HAH! SOON THIS DEVICE WILL CREATE A ZDARSIONIC-BURST THAT WILL BE AMPLIFIED BY THE STEEL STRUCTURE OF THIS SKYSCRAPER!
AND WHAT BETTER PLACE TO SET OFF THE DEVICE THAN METROPOLIS'S VERY OWN DAILY PLANET BUILDING?! HA HA HA HA HA!
HEH
FOOLISH EARTHLINGS! THE AMPLIFIED BURST WILL DESTROY EVERY ELECTRONIC DEVICE ON THE PLANET! NO MORE TELEPHONES, PLANES, AUTOMOBILES,TELEVISIONS OR COMPUTERS... NO MORE CDS, DVDS, MPEGS OR MP3S... NO MORE AVRIL!
LIFT
OPEN HERE
KEVIN, I THINK IT'S TIME WE SWAT SOME BUGS!
YOU SAID IT! HEY, ALIENS—THIS IS A RAID!
WELL, WELL! FOR LITTLE NUISANCES, YOU'RE SURE A PAIR OF BIG BLOWHARDS!
HEH.
COME ON, LACKEYS—LET'S SHOW THEM WE CAN BE EVEN BIGGER BLOWHARDS...WITH A VENGEANCE! HA HA HA HA HA!
FLAP
FLAP
FLAP
FLAP
SLAM!
WHOOSH!
UGH!
WHOOOOSH!
SUPERDOG! ARE YOU OKAY, BOY?
I-I THINK SO, BUT IT FEELS LIKE SOMETHING IS SAPPING MY ENERGY...
...BUT NEVER MIND! WE'VE GOT TO DESTROY THAT DEVICE!

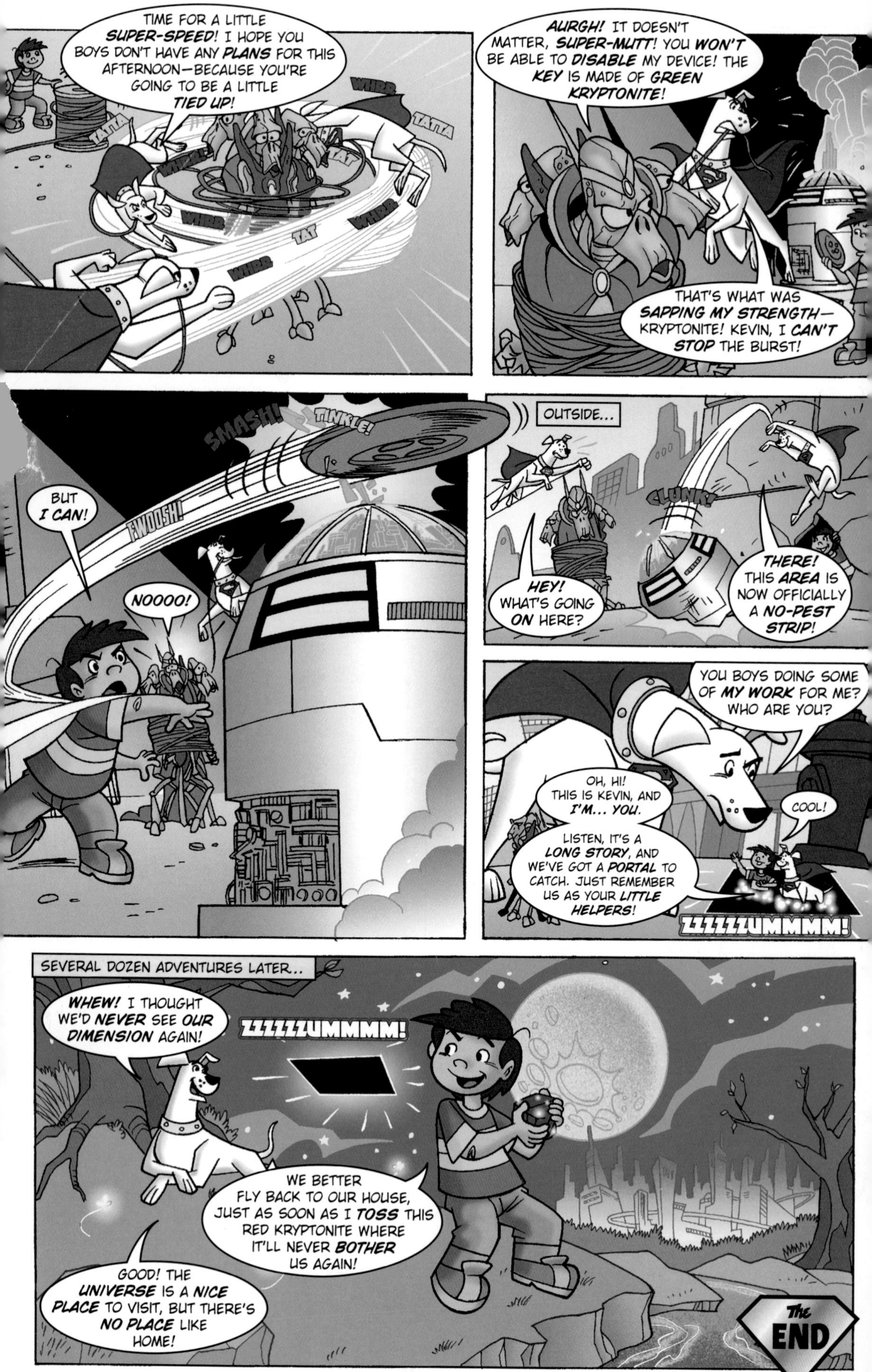
TIME FOR A LITTLE SUPER-SPEED! I HOPE YOU BOYS DON'T HAVE ANY PLANS FOR THIS AFTERNOON—BECAUSE YOU'RE GOING TO BE A LITTLE TIED UP!
WHRR
TATTA
TATTA
WHRR
TAT
WHRR
TAT
WHRR
WHRR
AURGH! IT DOESN'T MATTER, SUPER-MUTT! YOU WON'T BE ABLE TO DISABLE MY DEVICE! THE KEY IS MADE OF GREEN KRYPTONITE!
THAT'S WHAT WAS SAPPING MY STRENGTH—KRYPTONITE! KEVIN, I CAN'T STOP THE BURST!
SMASH!
TINKLE!
BUT I CAN!
FWOOSH!
NOOOO!
OUTSIDE...
CLUNK!
HEY! WHAT'S GOING ON HERE?
THERE! THIS AREA IS NOW OFFICIALLY A NO-PEST STRIP!
YOU BOYS DOING SOME OF MY WORK FOR ME? WHO ARE YOU?
OH, HI! THIS IS KEVIN, AND I'M... YOU.
COOL!
LISTEN, IT'S A LONG STORY, AND WE'VE GOT A PORTAL TO CATCH. JUST REMEMBER US AS YOUR LITTLE HELPERS!
ZZZZZZUMMMMM!
SEVERAL DOZEN ADVENTURES LATER...
WHEW! I THOUGHT WE'D NEVER SEE OUR DIMENSION AGAIN!
ZZZZZZUMMMMM!
WE BETTER FLY BACK TO OUR HOUSE, JUST AS SOON AS I TOSS THIS RED KRYPTONITE WHERE IT'LL NEVER BOTHER US AGAIN!
GOOD! THE UNIVERSE IS A NICE PLACE TO VISIT, BUT THERE'S NO PLACE LIKE HOME!
The END

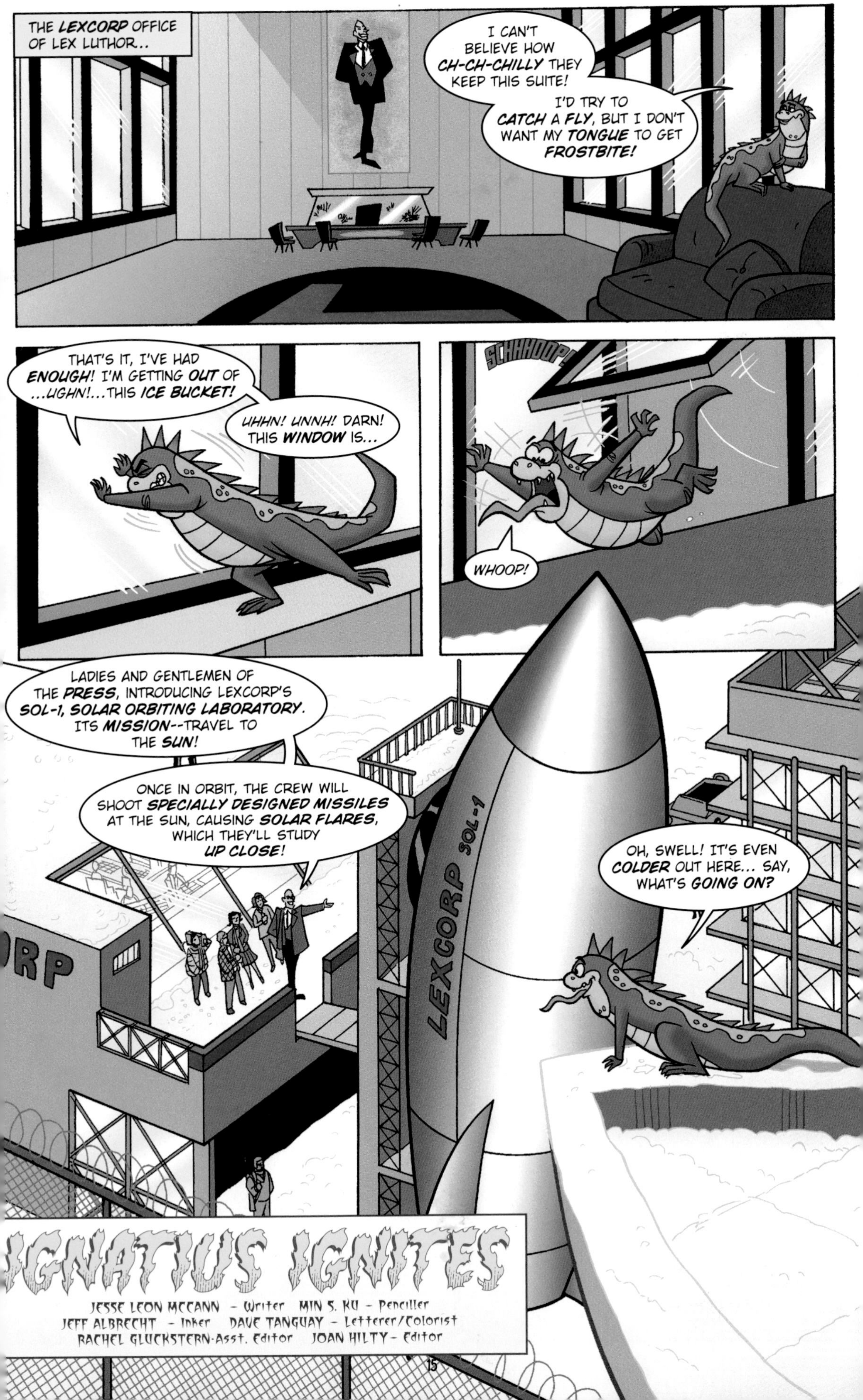

THE LEXCORP OFFICE OF LEX LUTHOR...
I CAN'T BELIEVE HOW CH-CH-CHILLY THEY KEEP THIS SUITE!
I'D TRY TO CATCH A FLY, BUT I DON'T WANT MY TONGUE TO GET FROSTBITE!
THAT'S IT, I'VE HAD ENOUGH! I'M GETTING OUT OF ...UGHN!...THIS ICE BUCKET!
UHHN! UNNH! DARN! THIS WINDOW IS...
SCHHHOOP!
WHOOP!
LADIES AND GENTLEMEN OF THE PRESS, INTRODUCING LEXCORP'S SOL-1, SOLAR ORBITING LABORATORY. ITS MISSION--TRAVEL TO THE SUN!
ONCE IN ORBIT, THE CREW WILL SHOOT SPECIALLY DESIGNED MISSILES AT THE SUN, CAUSING SOLAR FLARES, WHICH THEY'LL STUDY UP CLOSE!
OH, SWELL! IT'S EVEN COLDER OUT HERE... SAY, WHAT'S GOING ON?
LEXCORP SOL-1
IGNATIUS IGNITES
JESSE LEON MCCANN – Writer MIN S. KU – Penciller
JEFF ALBRECHT – Inker DAVE TANGUAY – Letterer/Colorist
RACHEL GLUCKSTERN-Asst. Editor JOAN HILTY – Editor

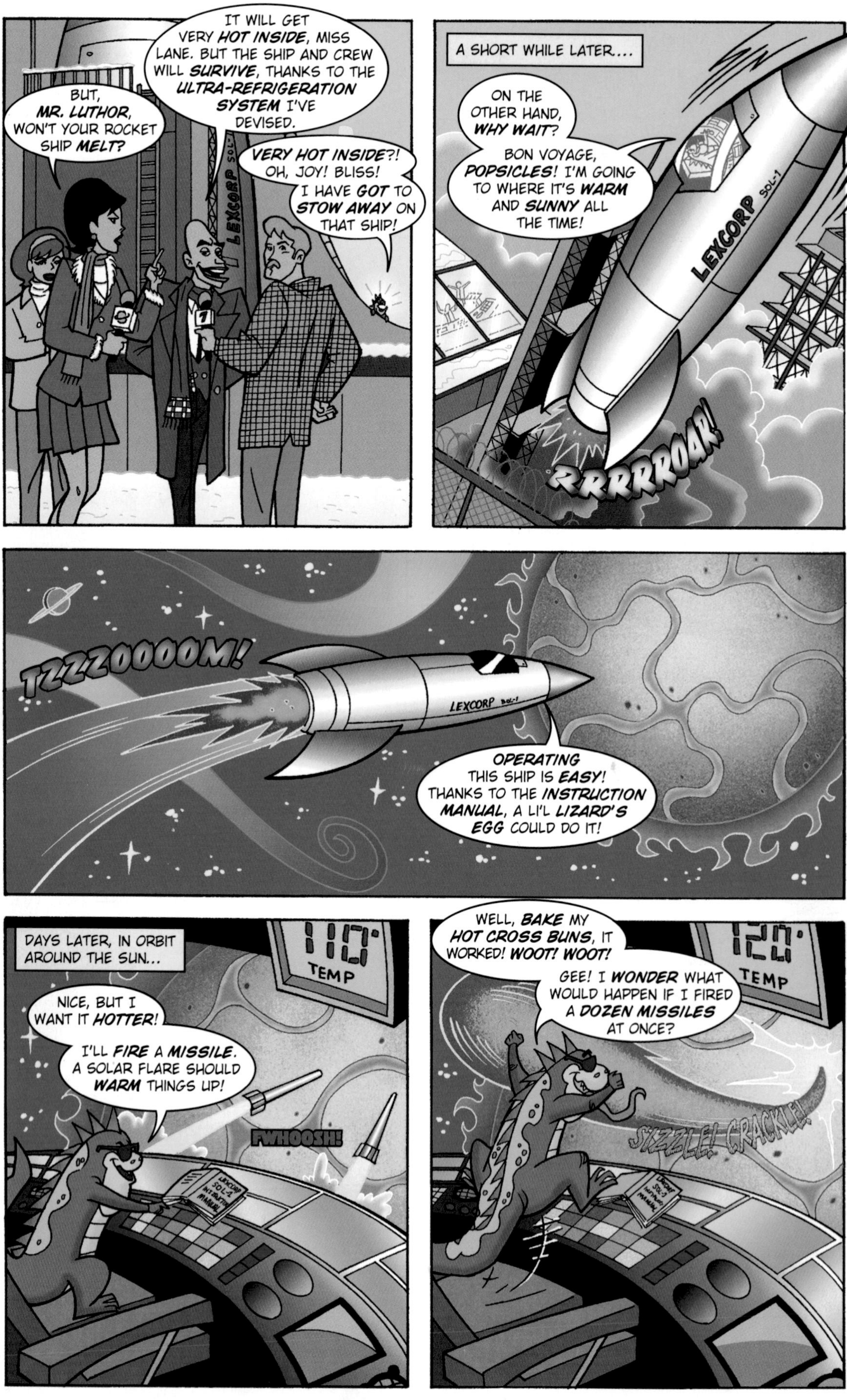
BUT, MR. LUTHOR, WON'T YOUR ROCKET SHIP MELT?
IT WILL GET VERY HOT INSIDE, MISS LANE. BUT THE SHIP AND CREW WILL SURVIVE, THANKS TO THE ULTRA-REFRIGERATION SYSTEM I'VE DEVISED.
VERY HOT INSIDE?! OH, JOY! BLISS! I HAVE GOT TO STOW AWAY ON THAT SHIP!
LEXCORP SOL-1
A SHORT WHILE LATER....
ON THE OTHER HAND, WHY WAIT?
BON VOYAGE, POPSICLES! I'M GOING TO WHERE IT'S WARM AND SUNNY ALL THE TIME!
LEXCORP SOL-1
RRRRROAR!
TZZZOOOOM!
LEXCORP SOL-1
OPERATING THIS SHIP IS EASY! THANKS TO THE INSTRUCTION MANUAL, A LI'L LIZARD'S EGG COULD DO IT!
DAYS LATER, IN ORBIT AROUND THE SUN...
110°
TEMP
NICE, BUT I WANT IT HOTTER!
I'LL FIRE A MISSILE. A SOLAR FLARE SHOULD WARM THINGS UP!
FWHOOSH!
WELL, BAKE MY HOT CROSS BUNS, IT WORKED! WOOT! WOOT!
120°
TEMP
GEE! I WONDER WHAT WOULD HAPPEN IF I FIRED A DOZEN MISSILES AT ONCE?
SIZZLE! CRACKLE!

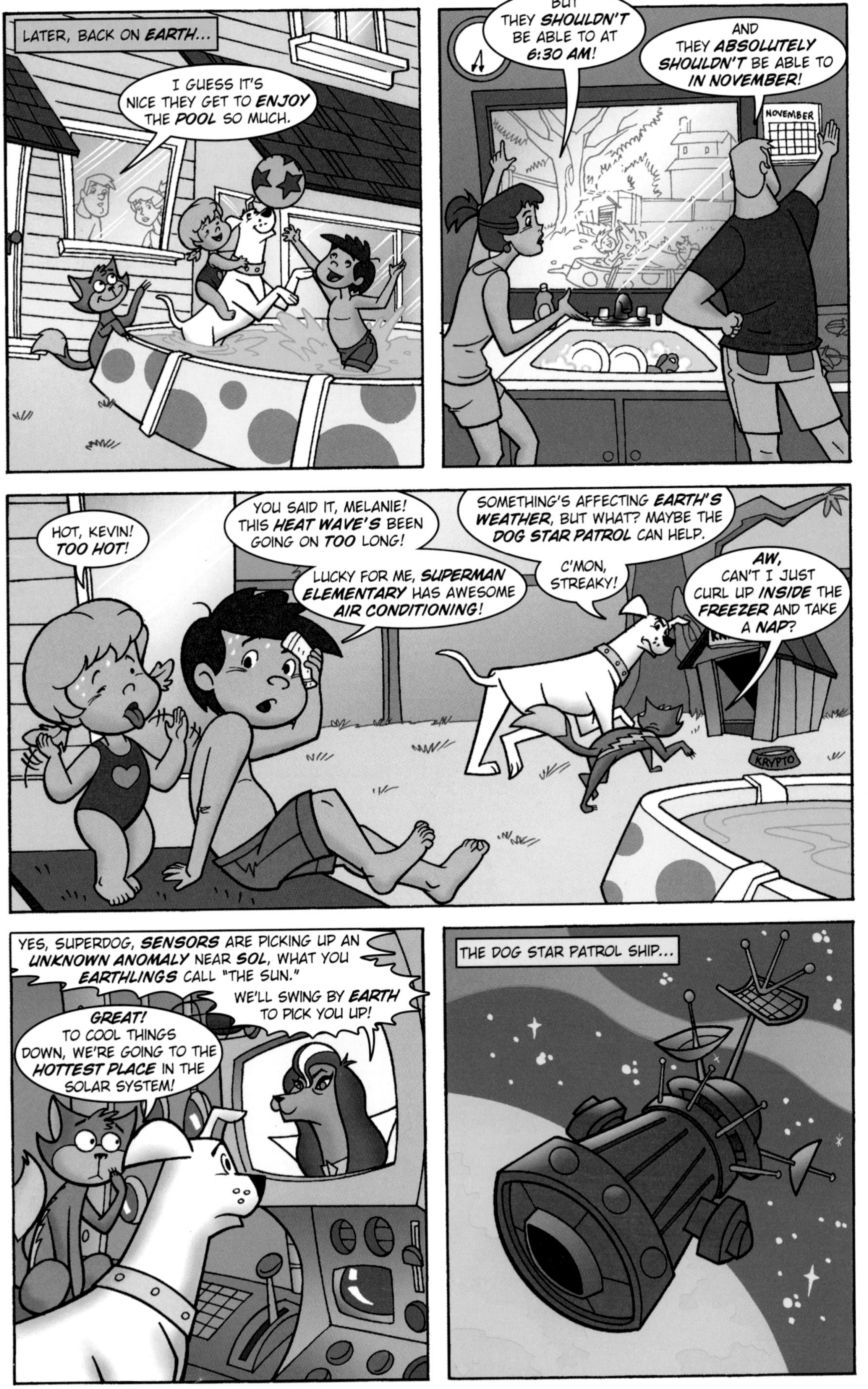

LATER, BACK ON EARTH...
I GUESS IT'S NICE THEY GET TO ENJOY THE POOL SO MUCH.
BUT THEY SHOULDN'T BE ABLE TO AT 6:30 AM!
AND THEY ABSOLUTELY SHOULDN'T BE ABLE TO IN NOVEMBER!
NOVEMBER
HOT, KEVIN! TOO HOT!
YOU SAID IT, MELANIE! THIS HEAT WAVE'S BEEN GOING ON TOO LONG!
LUCKY FOR ME, SUPERMAN ELEMENTARY HAS AWESOME AIR CONDITIONING!
SOMETHING'S AFFECTING EARTH'S WEATHER, BUT WHAT? MAYBE THE DOG STAR PATROL CAN HELP.
C'MON, STREAKY!
AW, CAN'T I JUST CURL UP INSIDE THE FREEZER AND TAKE A NAP?
KRYPTO
YES, SUPERDOG, SENSORS ARE PICKING UP AN UNKNOWN ANOMALY NEAR SOL, WHAT YOU EARTHLINGS CALL "THE SUN."
WE'LL SWING BY EARTH TO PICK YOU UP!
GREAT! TO COOL THINGS DOWN, WE'RE GOING TO THE HOTTEST PLACE IN THE SOLAR SYSTEM!
THE DOG STAR PATROL SHIP...

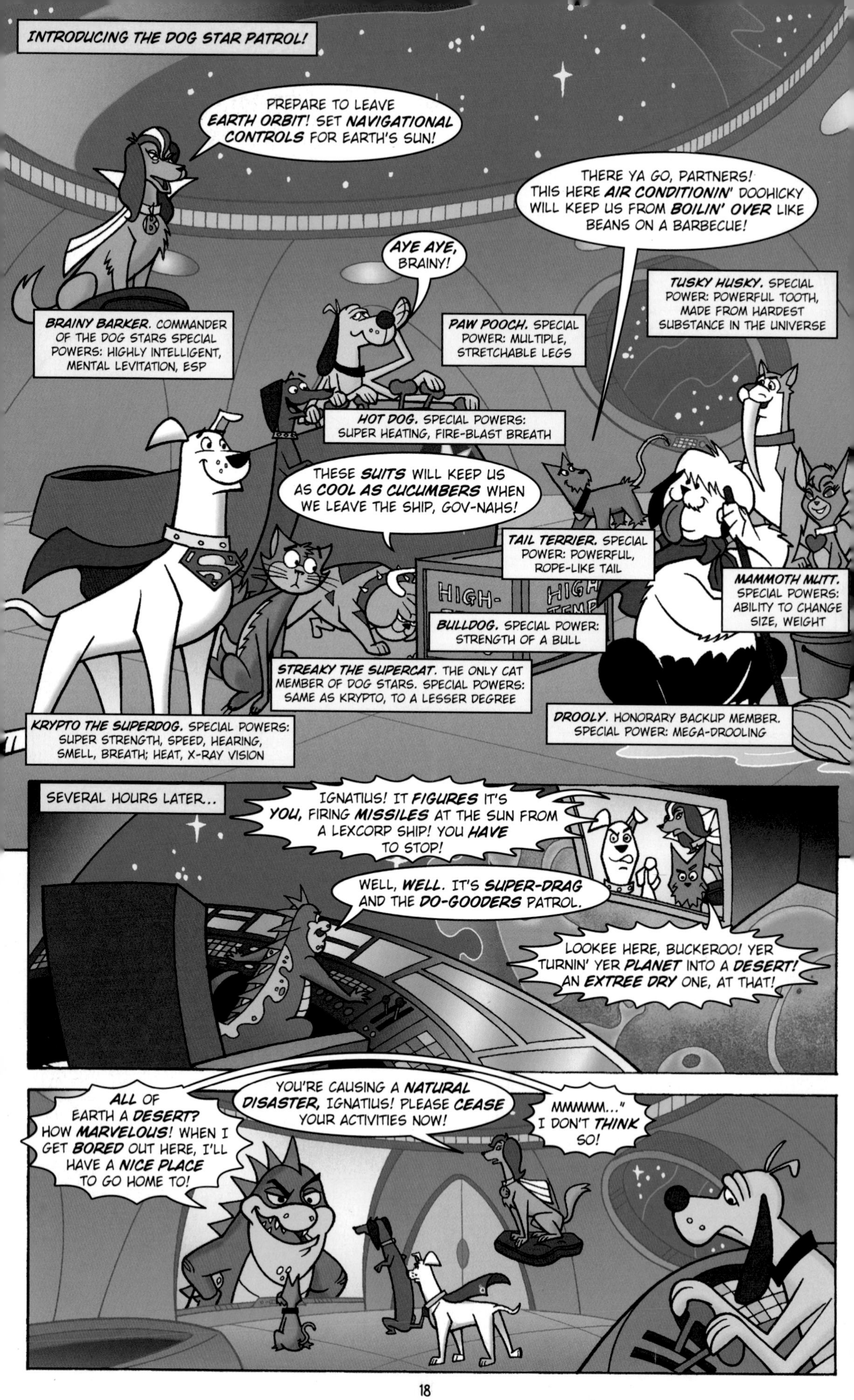

INTRODUCING THE DOG STAR PATROL!
PREPARE TO LEAVE EARTH ORBIT! SET NAVIGATIONAL CONTROLS FOR EARTH'S SUN!
THERE YA GO, PARTNERS! THIS HERE AIR CONDITIONIN' DOOHICKY WILL KEEP US FROM BOILIN' OVER LIKE BEANS ON A BARBECUE!
AYE AYE, BRAINY!
BRAINY BARKER. COMMANDER OF THE DOG STARS SPECIAL POWERS: HIGHLY INTELLIGENT, MENTAL LEVITATION, ESP
PAW POOCH. SPECIAL POWER: MULTIPLE, STRETCHABLE LEGS
TUSKY HUSKY. SPECIAL POWER: POWERFUL TOOTH, MADE FROM HARDEST SUBSTANCE IN THE UNIVERSE
HOT DOG. SPECIAL POWERS: SUPER HEATING, FIRE-BLAST BREATH
THESE SUITS WILL KEEP US AS COOL AS CUCUMBERS WHEN WE LEAVE THE SHIP, GOV-NAHS!
TAIL TERRIER. SPECIAL POWER: POWERFUL, ROPE-LIKE TAIL
MAMMOTH MUTT. SPECIAL POWERS: ABILITY TO CHANGE SIZE, WEIGHT
BULLDOG. SPECIAL POWER: STRENGTH OF A BULL
STREAKY THE SUPERCAT. THE ONLY CAT MEMBER OF DOG STARS. SPECIAL POWERS: SAME AS KRYPTO, TO A LESSER DEGREE
KRYPTO THE SUPERDOG. SPECIAL POWERS: SUPER STRENGTH, SPEED, HEARING, SMELL, BREATH; HEAT, X-RAY VISION
DROOLY. HONORARY BACKUP MEMBER. SPECIAL POWER: MEGA-DROOLING
SEVERAL HOURS LATER...
IGNATIUS! IT FIGURES IT'S YOU, FIRING MISSILES AT THE SUN FROM A LEXCORP SHIP! YOU HAVE TO STOP!
WELL, WELL. IT'S SUPER-DRAG AND THE DO-GOODERS PATROL.
LOOKEE HERE, BUCKEROO! YER TURNIN' YER PLANET INTO A DESERT! AN EXTREE DRY ONE, AT THAT!
ALL OF EARTH A DESERT? HOW MARVELOUS! WHEN I GET BORED OUT HERE, I'LL HAVE A NICE PLACE TO GO HOME TO!
YOU'RE CAUSING A NATURAL DISASTER, IGNATIUS! PLEASE CEASE YOUR ACTIVITIES NOW!
MMMMM..." I DON'T THINK SO!

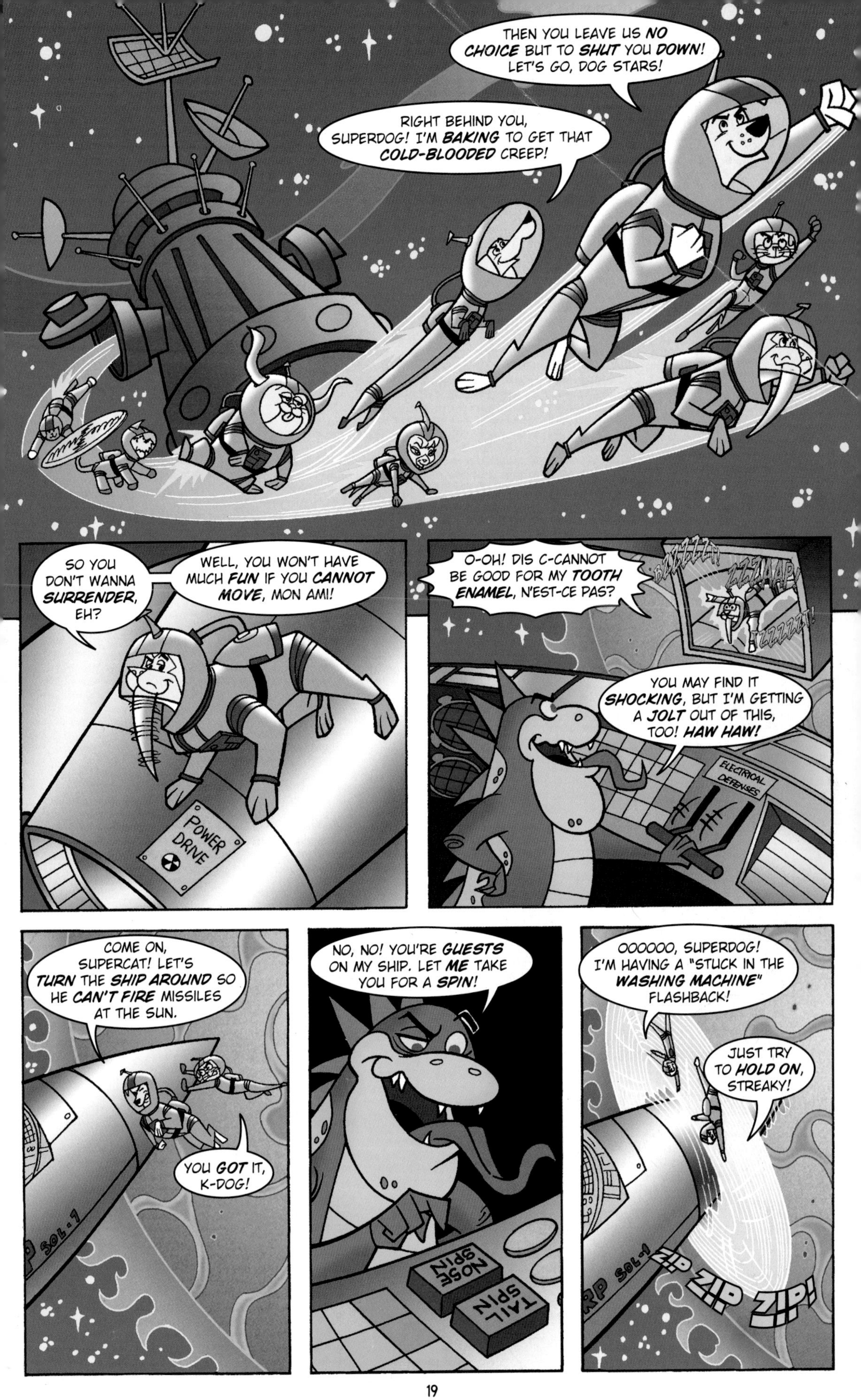
THEN YOU LEAVE US NO CHOICE BUT TO SHUT YOU DOWN! LET'S GO, DOG STARS!
RIGHT BEHIND YOU, SUPERDOG! I'M BAKING TO GET THAT COLD-BLOODED CREEP!
SO YOU DON'T WANNA SURRENDER, EH?
WELL, YOU WON'T HAVE MUCH FUN IF YOU CANNOT MOVE, MON AMI!
POWER DRIVE
O-OH! DIS C-CANNOT BE GOOD FOR MY TOOTH ENAMEL, N'EST-CE PAS?
YOU MAY FIND IT SHOCKING, BUT I'M GETTING A JOLT OUT OF THIS, TOO! HAW HAW!
ELECTRICAL DEFENSES
COME ON, SUPERCAT! LET'S TURN THE SHIP AROUND SO HE CAN'T FIRE MISSILES AT THE SUN.
YOU GOT IT, K-DOG!
SOL-1
NO, NO! YOU'RE GUESTS ON MY SHIP. LET ME TAKE YOU FOR A SPIN!
NOSE SPIN
TAIL SPIN
OOOOOO, SUPERDOG! I'M HAVING A "STUCK IN THE WASHING MACHINE" FLASHBACK!
JUST TRY TO HOLD ON, STREAKY!
SOL-1
ZIP ZIP ZIP!

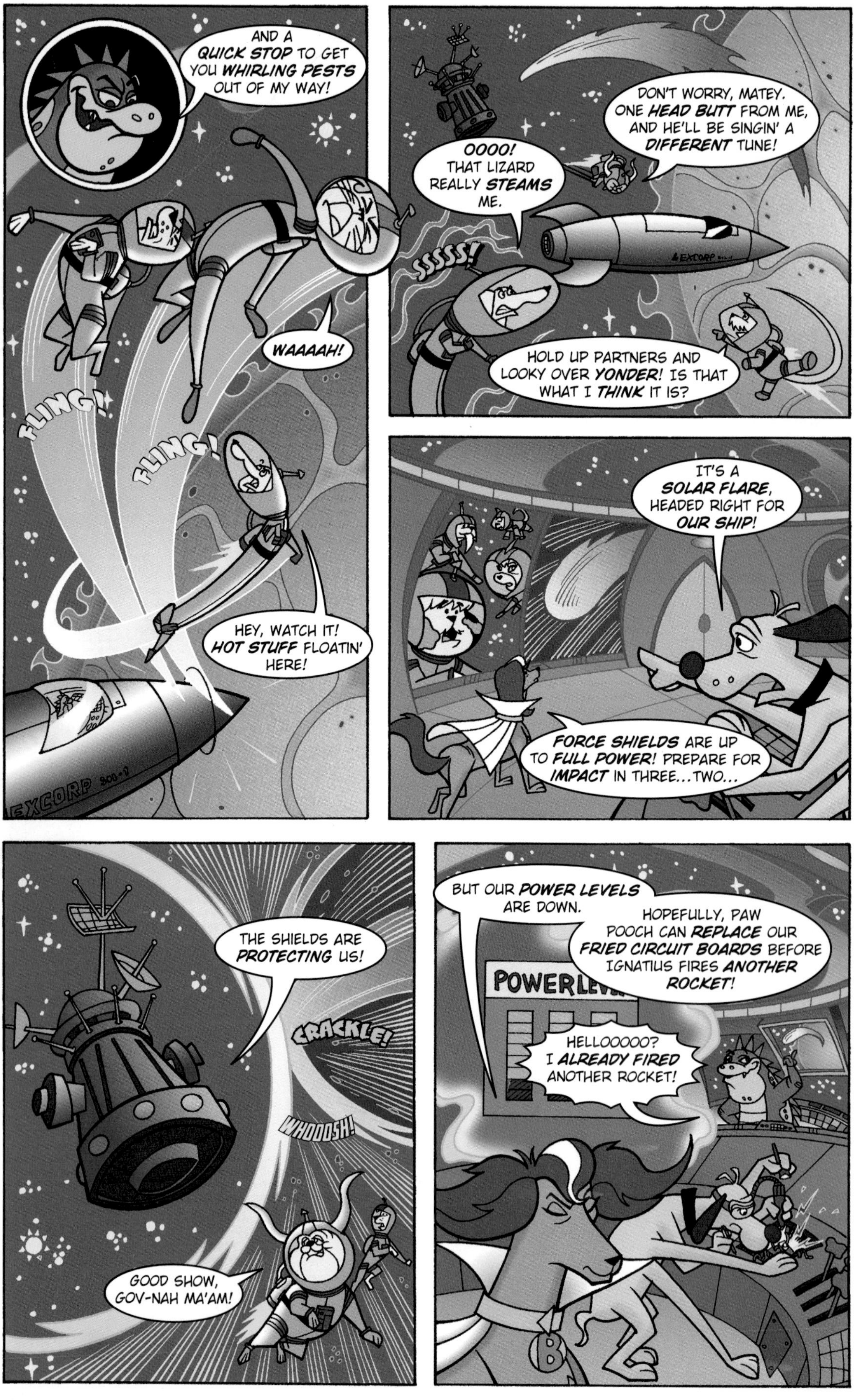
AND A QUICK STOP TO GET YOU WHIRLING PESTS OUT OF MY WAY!
WAAAAH!
FLING!!
FLING!
HEY, WATCH IT! HOT STUFF FLOATIN' HERE!
EXCORP
OOOO! THAT LIZARD REALLY STEAMS ME.
SSSSS!
DON'T WORRY, MATEY. ONE HEAD BUTT FROM ME, AND HE'LL BE SINGIN' A DIFFERENT TUNE!
HOLD UP PARTNERS AND LOOKY OVER YONDER! IS THAT WHAT I THINK IT IS?
IT'S A SOLAR FLARE, HEADED RIGHT FOR OUR SHIP!
FORCE SHIELDS ARE UP TO FULL POWER! PREPARE FOR IMPACT IN THREE...TWO...
THE SHIELDS ARE PROTECTING US!
CRACKLE!
WHOOOSH!
GOOD SHOW, GOV-NAH MA'AM!
BUT OUR POWER LEVELS ARE DOWN.
HOPEFULLY, PAW POOCH CAN REPLACE OUR FRIED CIRCUIT BOARDS BEFORE IGNATIUS FIRES ANOTHER ROCKET!
POWER LEVEL
HELLOOOOO? I ALREADY FIRED ANOTHER ROCKET!

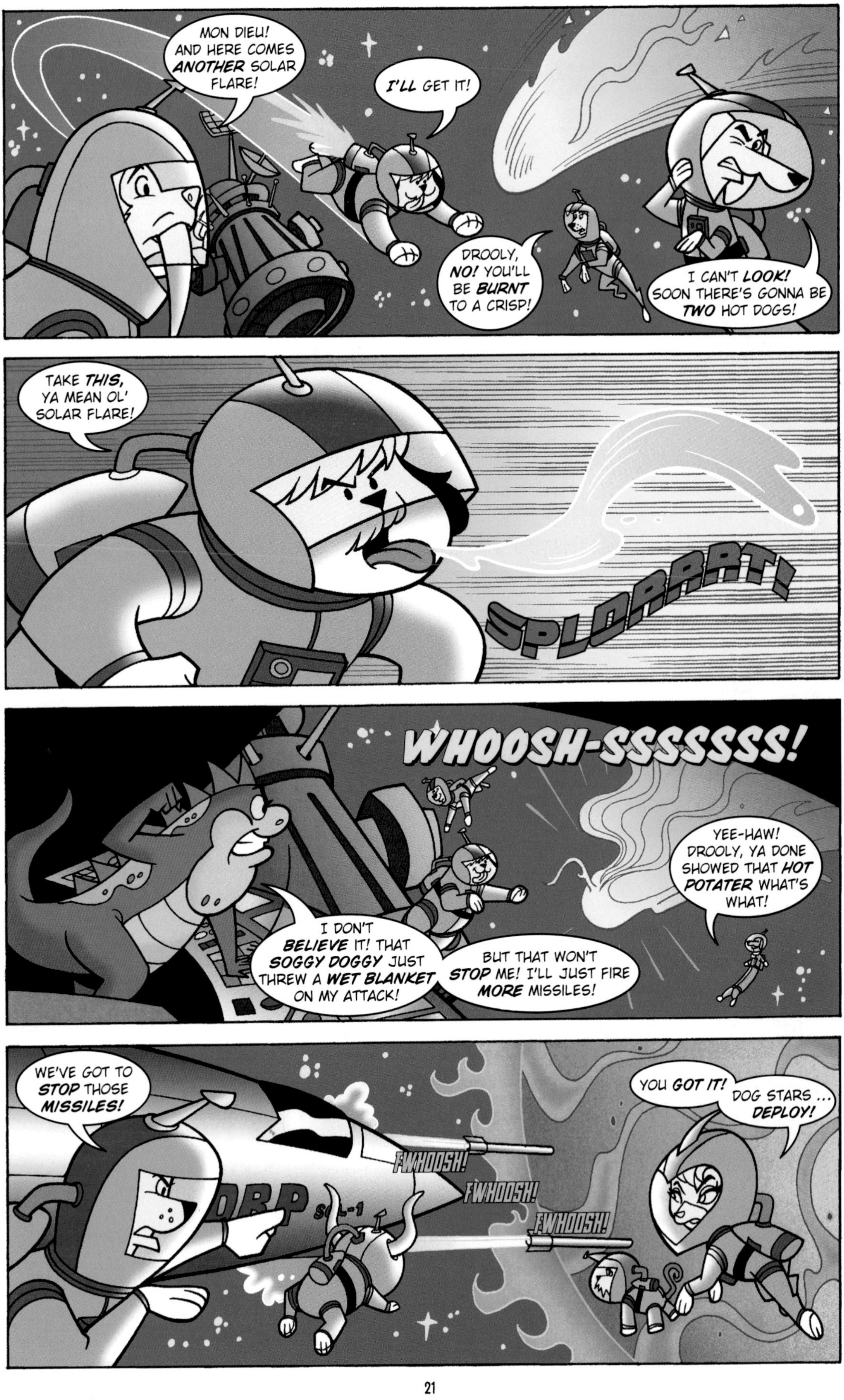
MON DIEU! AND HERE COMES ANOTHER SOLAR FLARE!
I'LL GET IT!
DROOLY, NO! YOU'LL BE BURNT TO A CRISP!
I CAN'T LOOK! SOON THERE'S GONNA BE TWO HOT DOGS!
TAKE THIS, YA MEAN OL' SOLAR FLARE!
SPLORRRT!
WHOOSH-SSSSSS!
YEE-HAW! DROOLY, YA DONE SHOWED THAT HOT POTATER WHAT'S WHAT!
I DON'T BELIEVE IT! THAT SOGGY DOGGY JUST THREW A WET BLANKET ON MY ATTACK!
BUT THAT WON'T STOP ME! I'LL JUST FIRE MORE MISSILES!
WE'VE GOT TO STOP THOSE MISSILES!
FWHOOSH!
FWHOOSH!
FWHOOSH!
YOU GOT IT!
DOG STARS ... DEPLOY!

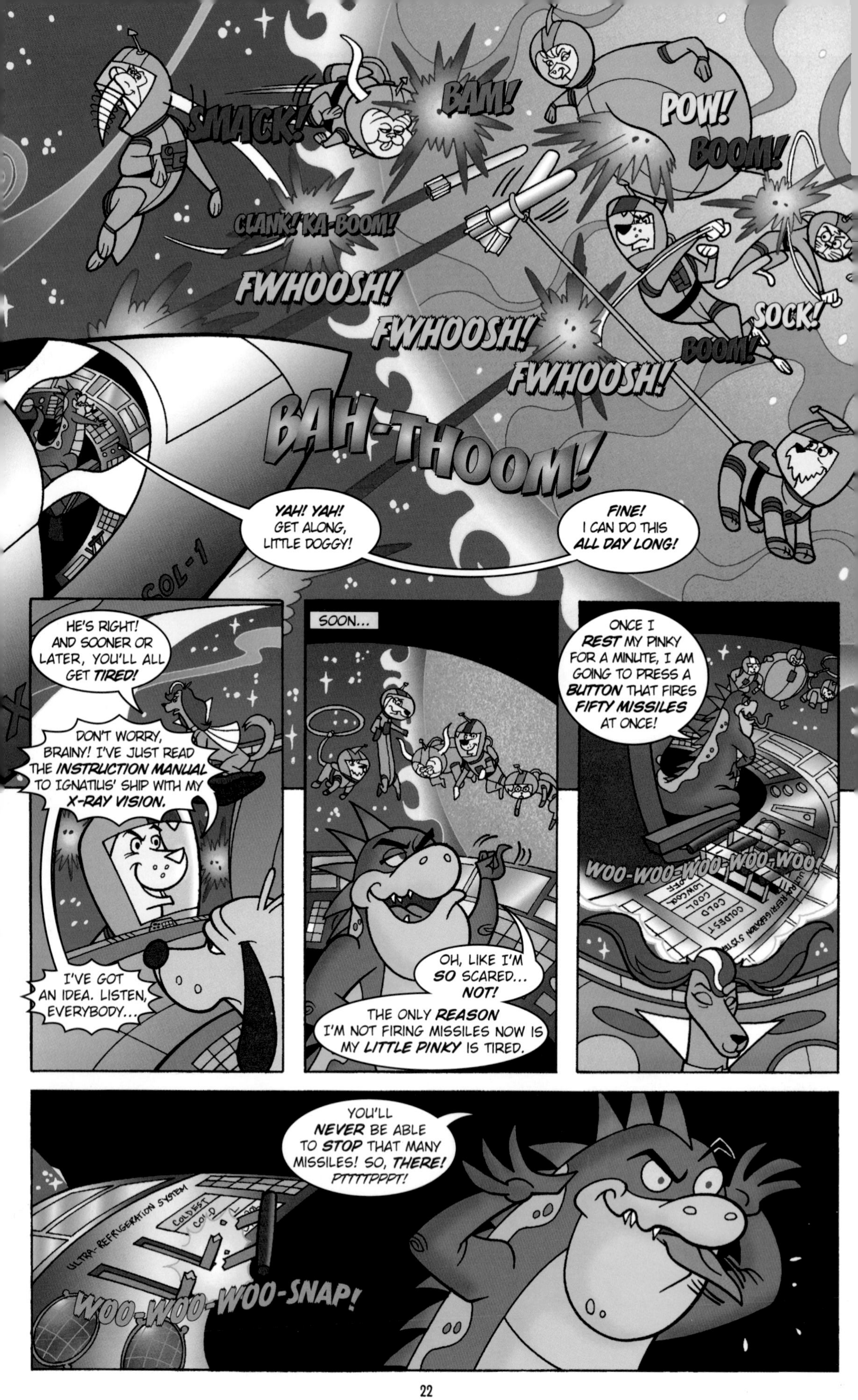
SMACK!
BAM!
POW!
BOOM!
CLANK! KA-BOOM!
FWHOOSH!
FWHOOSH!
SOCK!
BOOM!
FWHOOSH!
BAH-THOOM!
YAH! YAH! GET ALONG, LITTLE DOGGY!
FINE! I CAN DO THIS ALL DAY LONG!
COL-1
HE'S RIGHT! AND SOONER OR LATER, YOU'LL ALL GET TIRED!
DON'T WORRY, BRAINY! I'VE JUST READ THE INSTRUCTION MANUAL TO IGNATIUS' SHIP WITH MY X-RAY VISION.
I'VE GOT AN IDEA. LISTEN, EVERYBODY...
SOON...
OH, LIKE I'M SO SCARED... NOT!
THE ONLY REASON I'M NOT FIRING MISSILES NOW IS MY LITTLE PINKY IS TIRED.
ONCE I REST MY PINKY FOR A MINUTE, I AM GOING TO PRESS A BUTTON THAT FIRES FIFTY MISSILES AT ONCE!
WOO-WOO-WOO-WOO-WOO!
YOU'LL NEVER BE ABLE TO STOP THAT MANY MISSILES! SO, THERE! PTTTTPPPT!
ULTRA-REFRIGERATION SYSTEM
COLDEST
COLD
WOO-WOO-WOO-SNAP!

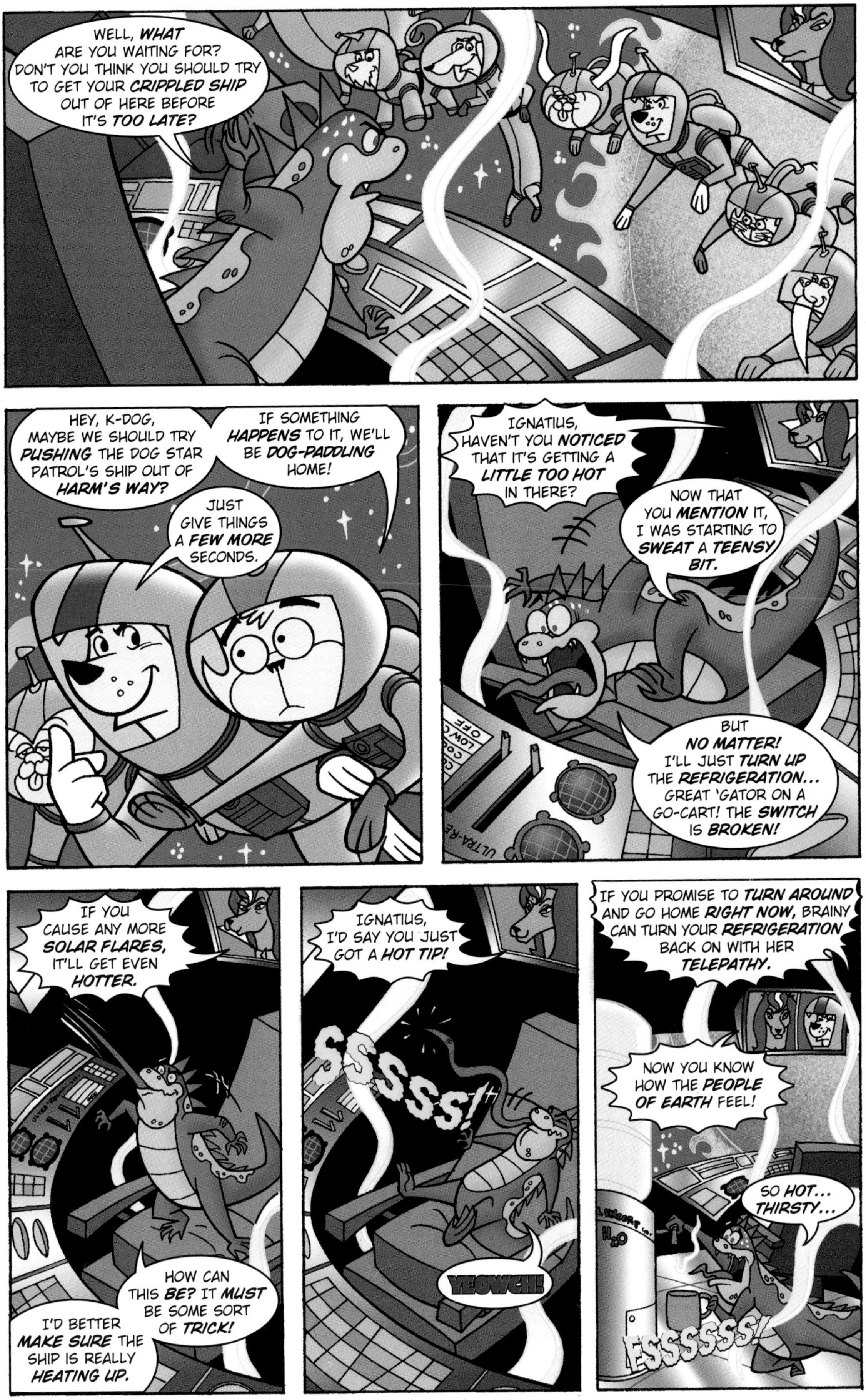
WELL, WHAT ARE YOU WAITING FOR? DON'T YOU THINK YOU SHOULD TRY TO GET YOUR CRIPPLED SHIP OUT OF HERE BEFORE IT'S TOO LATE?
HEY, K-DOG, MAYBE WE SHOULD TRY PUSHING THE DOG STAR PATROL'S SHIP OUT OF HARM'S WAY?
IF SOMETHING HAPPENS TO IT, WE'LL BE DOG-PADDLING HOME!
JUST GIVE THINGS A FEW MORE SECONDS.
IGNATIUS, HAVEN'T YOU NOTICED THAT IT'S GETTING A LITTLE TOO HOT IN THERE?
NOW THAT YOU MENTION IT, I WAS STARTING TO SWEAT A TEENSY BIT.
BUT NO MATTER! I'LL JUST TURN UP THE REFRIGERATION... GREAT 'GATOR ON A GO-CART! THE SWITCH IS BROKEN!
IF YOU CAUSE ANY MORE SOLAR FLARES, IT'LL GET EVEN HOTTER.
I'D BETTER MAKE SURE THE SHIP IS REALLY HEATING UP.
HOW CAN THIS BE? IT MUST BE SOME SORT OF TRICK!
IGNATIUS, I'D SAY YOU JUST GOT A HOT TIP!
SSSSS!
YEOWCH!
IF YOU PROMISE TO TURN AROUND AND GO HOME RIGHT NOW, BRAINY CAN TURN YOUR REFRIGERATION BACK ON WITH HER TELEPATHY.
NOW YOU KNOW HOW THE PEOPLE OF EARTH FEEL!
SO HOT... THIRSTY...
FSSSSSSS!

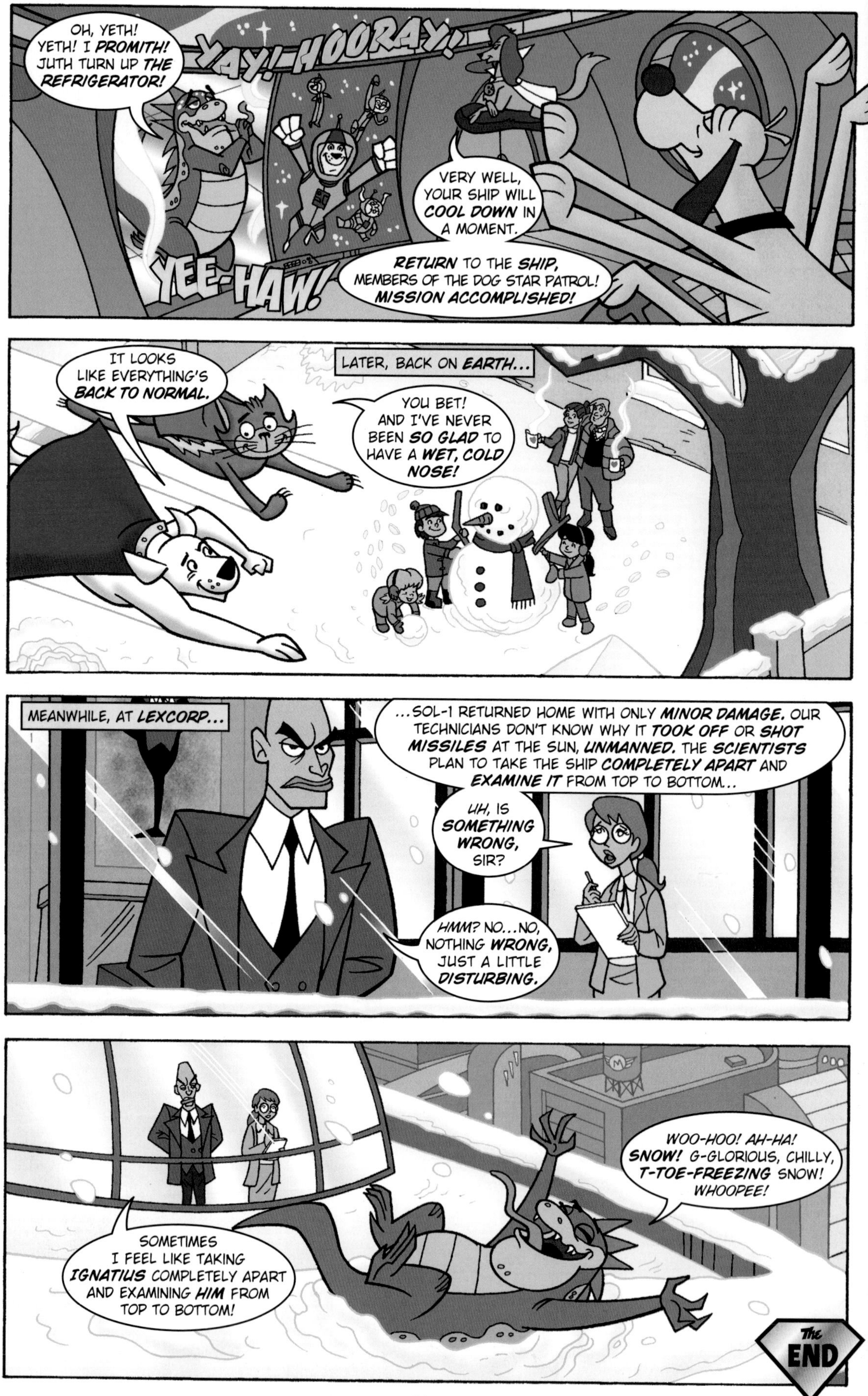

OH, YETH! YETH! I PROMITH! JUTH TURN UP THE REFRIGERATOR!
YAY! HOORAY!
YEE-HAW!
VERY WELL, YOUR SHIP WILL COOL DOWN IN A MOMENT.
RETURN TO THE SHIP, MEMBERS OF THE DOG STAR PATROL! MISSION ACCOMPLISHED!
LATER, BACK ON EARTH...
IT LOOKS LIKE EVERYTHING'S BACK TO NORMAL.
YOU BET! AND I'VE NEVER BEEN SO GLAD TO HAVE A WET, COLD NOSE!
MEANWHILE, AT LEXCORP...
...SOL-1 RETURNED HOME WITH ONLY MINOR DAMAGE. OUR TECHNICIANS DON'T KNOW WHY IT TOOK OFF OR SHOT MISSILES AT THE SUN, UNMANNED. THE SCIENTISTS PLAN TO TAKE THE SHIP COMPLETELY APART AND EXAMINE IT FROM TOP TO BOTTOM...
UH, IS SOMETHING WRONG, SIR?
HMM? NO...NO, NOTHING WRONG, JUST A LITTLE DISTURBING.
WOO-HOO! AH-HA! SNOW! G-GLORIOUS, CHILLY, T-TOE-FREEZING SNOW! WHOOPEE!
SOMETIMES I FEEL LIKE TAKING IGNATIUS COMPLETELY APART AND EXAMINING HIM FROM TOP TO BOTTOM!
The END

Superdog Jokes!

WHAT DID THE TIRED DOG SAY?

I'VE HAD A RUFF DAY!

WHAT DID THE DOG CATCHER SAY TO HIS DENTIST?

I HAVE A FEW LOOSE CANINES!

WHAT DID THE ABSENT DOG TEACHER ASK TO HAVE FOR HER CLASSROOM?

A SUB-WOOFER!

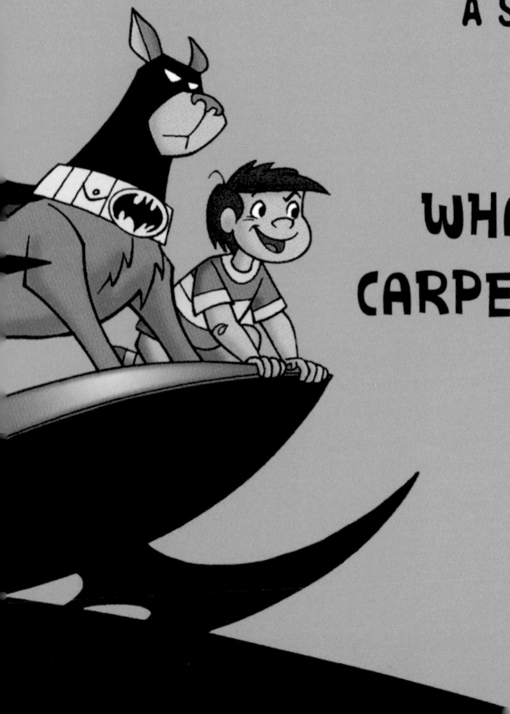

WHAT DID THE DOGGY CARPENTER SPECIALIZE IN?

ROOFING!

Creators

JESSE LEON MCCANN WRITER

Jesse Leon McCann is a *New York Times* Top-Ten Children's Book Writer, as well as a prolific all-ages comics writer. His credits include Pinky and the Brain, Animaniacs, and Looney Tunes for DC Comics; Scooby-Doo and Shrek 2 for Scholastic; and The Simpsons and Futurama for Bongo Comics. He lives in Los Angeles with his wife and four cats.

MIN SUNG KU PENCILLER

As a young child, Min Sung Ku dreamed of becoming a comic book illustrator. At six years old, he drew a picture of Superman standing behind the American flag. He has since achieved his childhood dream, having illustrated popular licensed comics properties like the Justice League, Batman Beyond, Spider-Man, Ben 10, Phineas & Ferb, the Replacements, the Proud Family, Krpyto the Superdog, and, of course, Superman. Min lives with his lovely wife and their beautiful twin daughters, Elisia and Eliana.

DAVE TANGUAY COLORIST/LETTERER

David Tanguay has over 20 years of experience in the comic book industry. He has worked as an editor, layout artist, colorist, and letterer. He has also done web design, and he taught computer graphics at the State University of New York.

Glossary

AMPLIFIED (AM-pli-fyed) – made something louder or stronger

BRANCH (BRANCH) – a part of a tree that grows out from the trunk, or a specific part of an organization

DIMENSION (duh-MEN-shuhn) – another space and time

DOMINATION (dom-i-NAY-shuhn) – total control

MELLOW (MEL-oh) – soft or calm

METEOR (MEE-tee-ur) – a piece of rock or metal from space that enters Earth's atmosphere at high speed, burns, and forms a streak of light as it falls to the earth

NUISANCES (NOO-suhnss-iz) – things or people that annoy and cause problems

PANIC (PAN-ik) – struck with sudden terror or fear

SUITE (SWEET) – a connected series of rooms to be used together, like a hotel suite

Visual Questions & Prompts

1. THE WORD "BRANCH" IN THIS PANEL HAS TWO MEANINGS. CAN YOU EXPLAIN BOTH OF THEM?

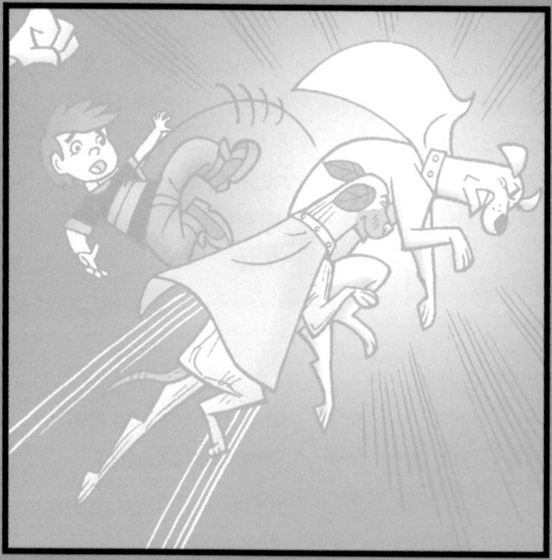

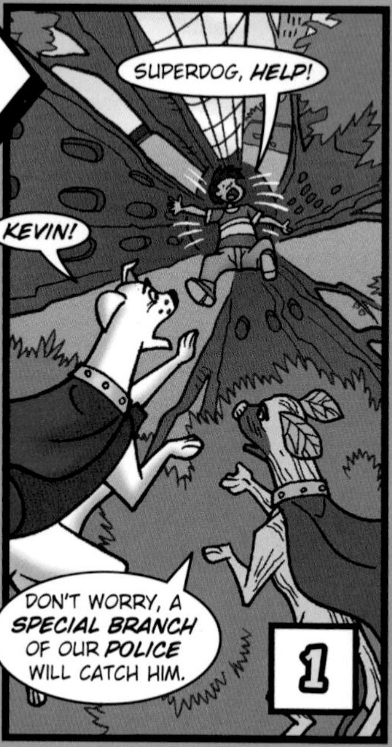

SUPERDOG, HELP!
KEVIN!
DON'T WORRY, A SPECIAL BRANCH OF OUR POLICE WILL CATCH HIM.
1

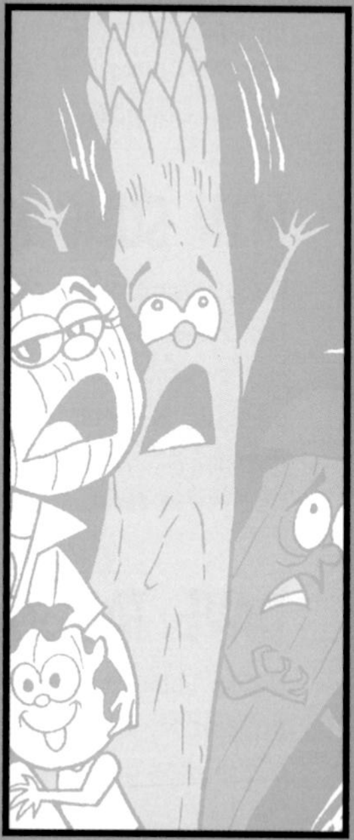

2. WHY DOES THE BACKGROUND IMAGE OF THIS PANEL HAVE SO MANY DIFFERENT IMAGES? EXPLAIN.

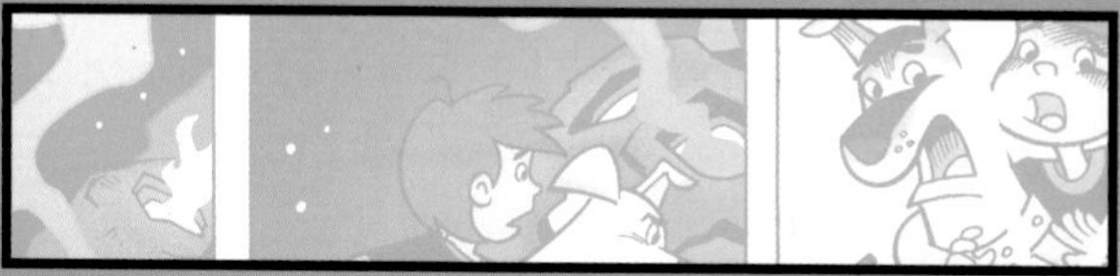

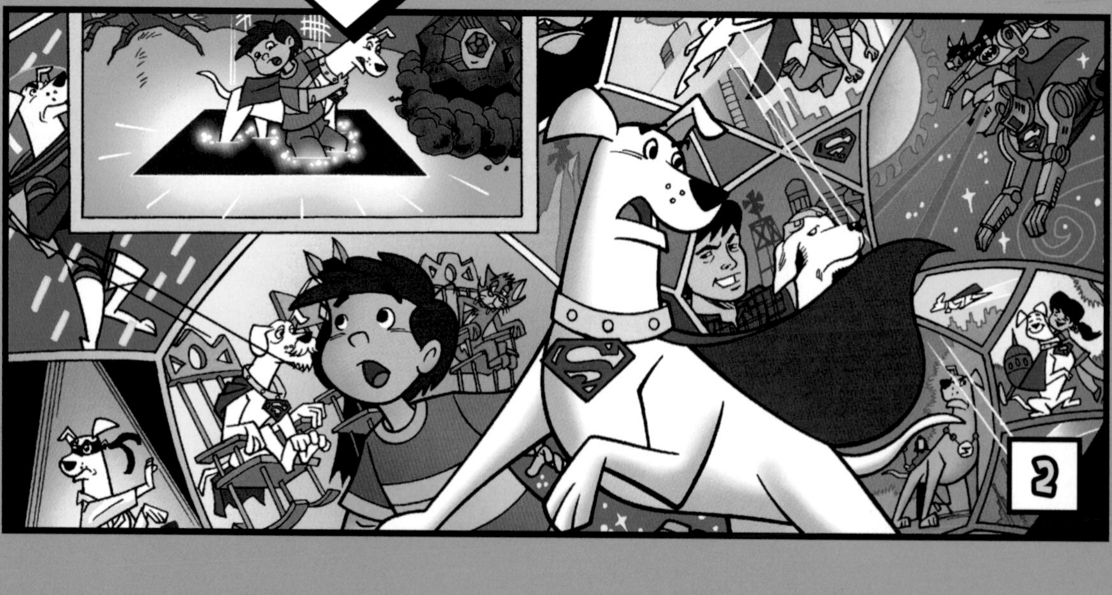

2

3. WHY DO YOU THINK THE ILLUSTRATOR ADDED LINES IN THE BACKGROUND OF THIS PANEL?

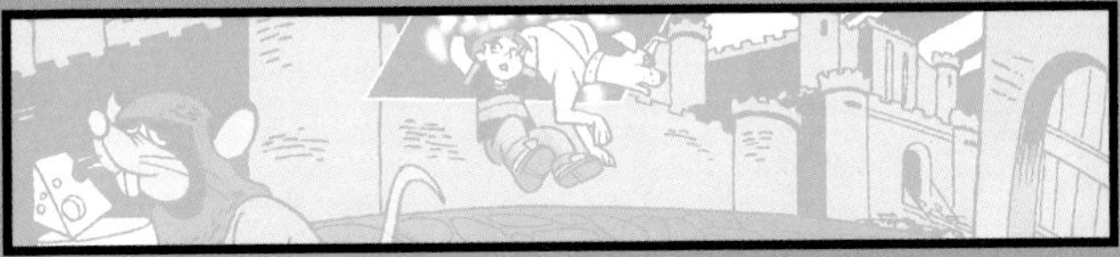

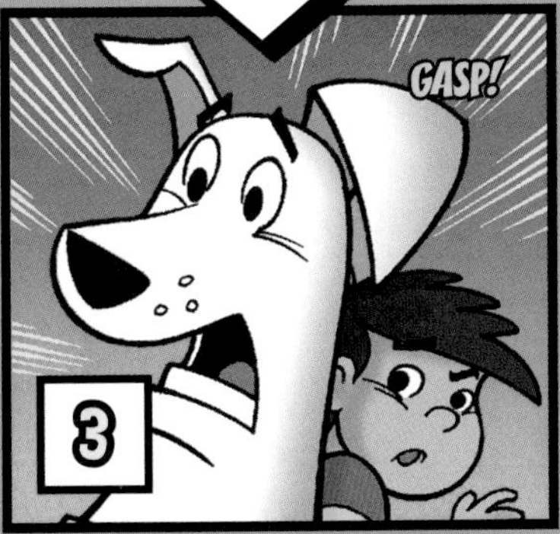
GASP!
3

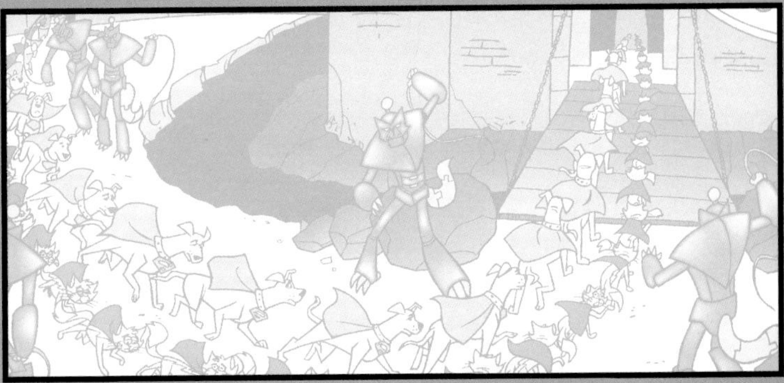

4. WHICH MEMBER OF THE DOG STAR PATROL IS YOUR FAVORITE? WHY? [SEE PAGE 18 FOR DETAILS.]

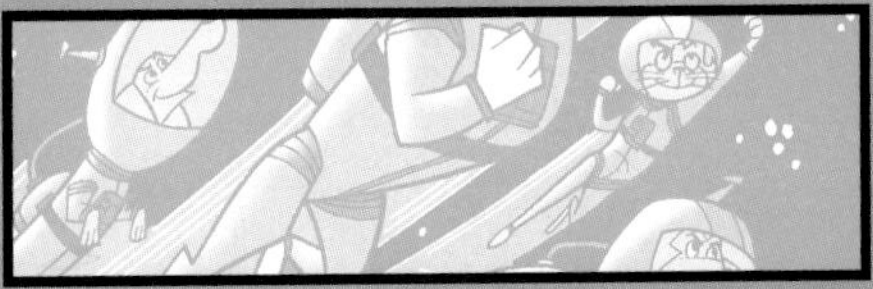

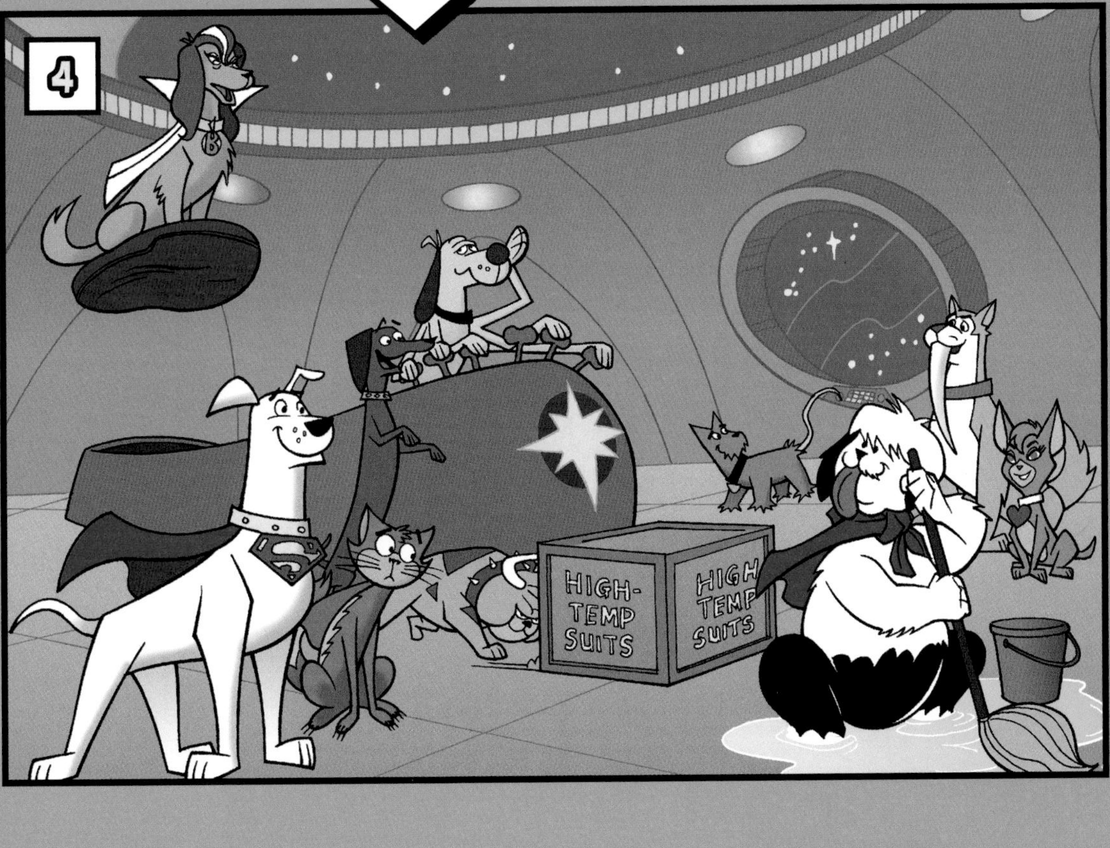
4
HIGH-TEMP SUITS
HIGH-TEMP SUITS

READ THEM ALL!

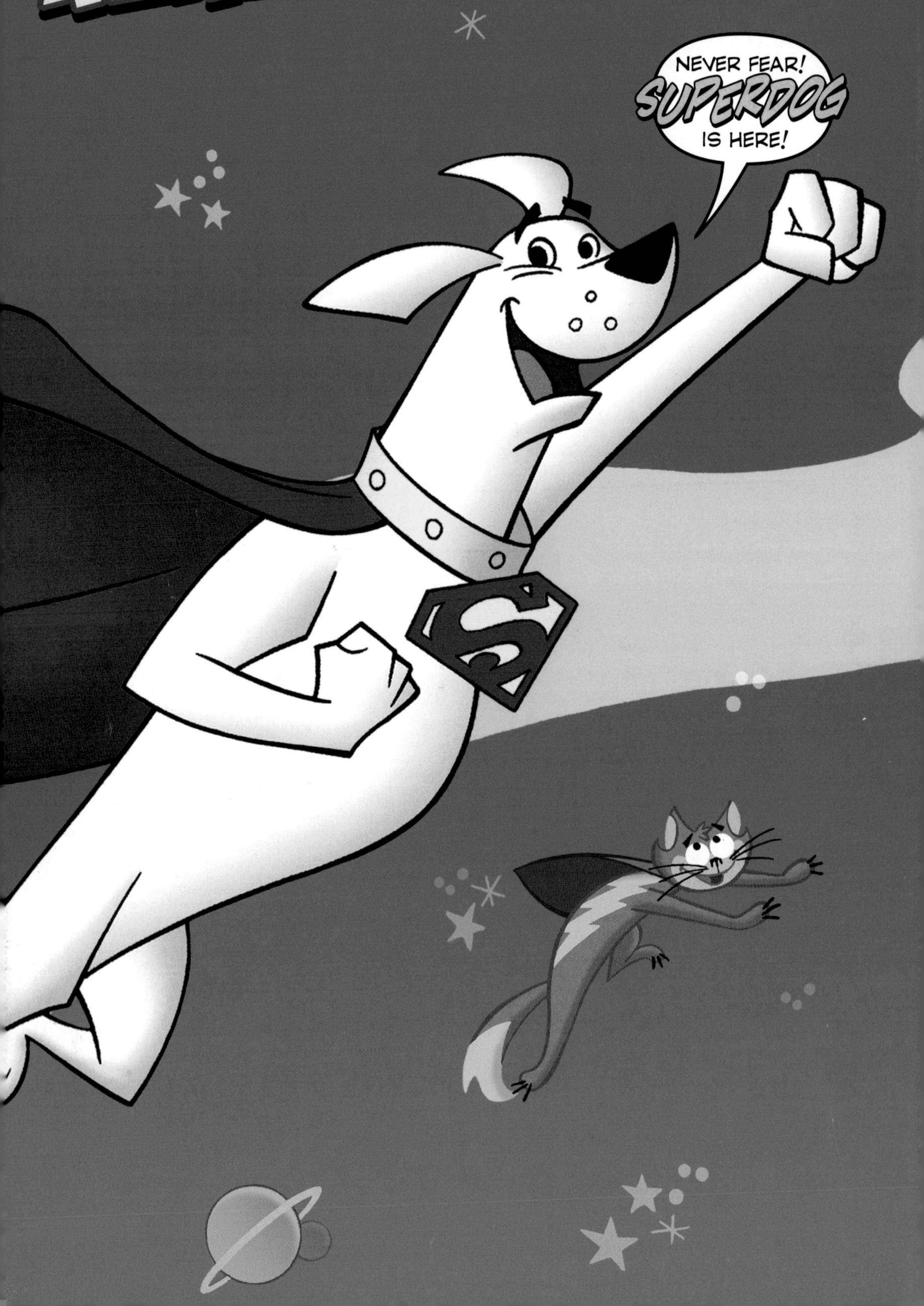
NEVER FEAR! SUPERDOG IS HERE!

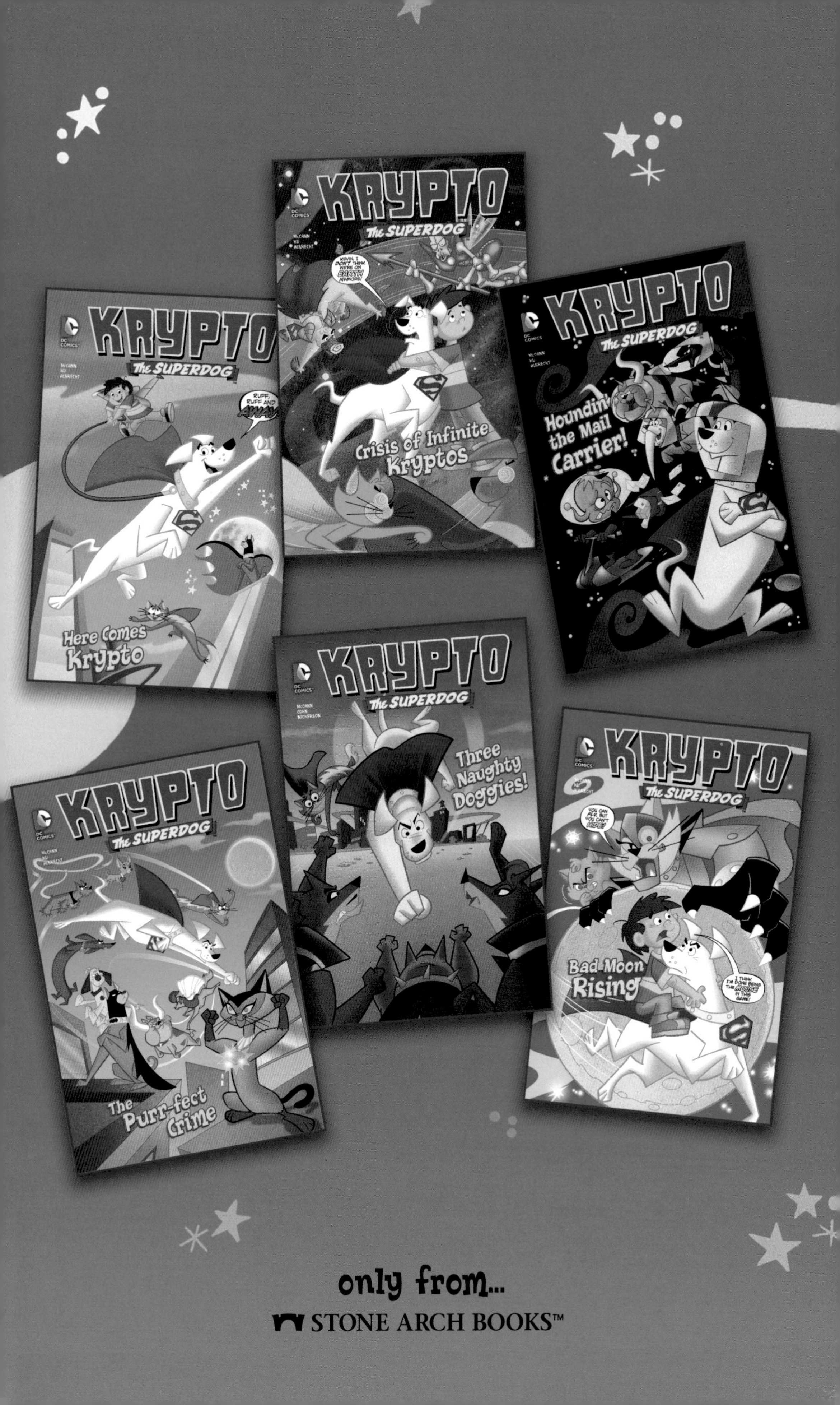
KRYPTO The SUPERDOG
RUFF, RUFF AND AWAY!
Here Comes Krypto
KRYPTO The SUPERDOG
KEVIN, I DON'T THINK WE'RE ON EARTH ANYMORE!
Crisis of Infinite Kryptos
KRYPTO The SUPERDOG
Hounding the Mail Carrier!
KRYPTO The SUPERDOG
The Purr-fect Crime
KRYPTO The SUPERDOG
Three Naughty Doggies!
KRYPTO The SUPERDOG
YOU CAN FLY, BUT YOU CAN'T HIDE!
Bad Moon Rising

KRYPTO
The SUPERDOG™

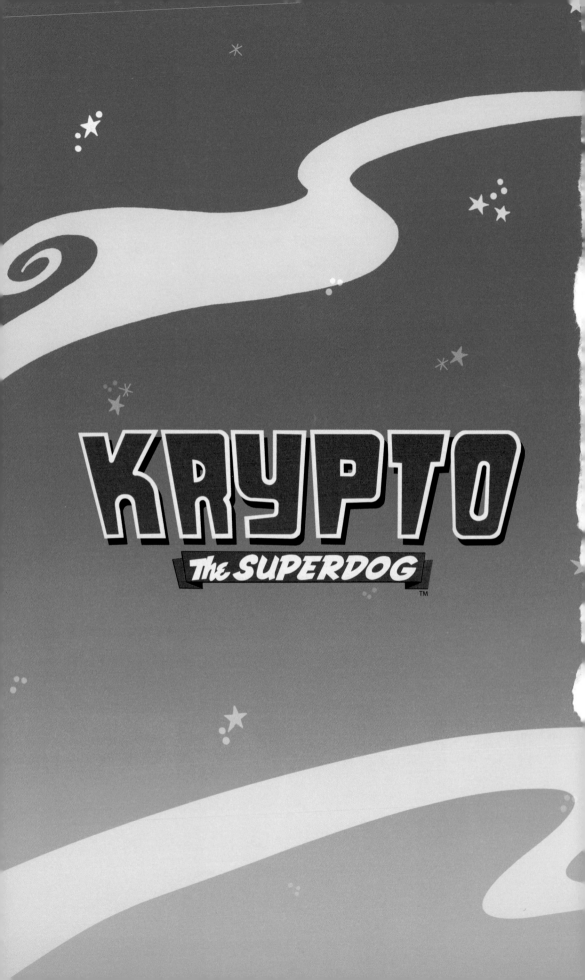